PENGUIN BOOKS
The Lion and the

Eric Arthur Blair (George Orwell) was born in 1903 in India, where his father worked for the Civil Service. The family moved to England in 1907 and in 1917 Orwell entered Eton, where he contributed regularly to the various college magazines. He left in 1921 and joined the Indian Imperial Police in Burma the following year. He resigned in 1928 having come to hate imperialism, as *Burmese Days* (1934) his first novel shows.

After this he lived for several years in poverty, at times among tramps, experiences which he relates in *Down and Out in Paris and London* (1933). For a time he worked as a schoolteacher but due to poor health he gave this up and worked as a part-time assistant in a Hampstead bookshop; later he was able to earn his living reviewing novels for the *New English Weekly*, a post he kept until 1940. In 1936 he visited areas of mass unemployment in Lancashire and Yorkshire and *The Road to Wigan Pier* (1937) is a powerful description of the poverty he saw there. At the end of 1936 Orwell went to Spain to fight for the Republicans and was wounded; his account of the civil war, *Homage to Catalonia*, is considered by many to be his greatest achievement. During the Second World War he was a member of the Home Guard and worked for the BBC Eastern Service from 1940 to 1943. As literary editor of *Tribune* he contributed a regular page of political and literary commentary. From 1945 Orwell was the *Observer*'s war correspondent and later became a regular contributor to the *Manchester Evening News*. His unique political allegory, *Animal Farm* was published in 1945, and it was this novel, together with *Nineteen Eighty-Four* (1949), which brought Orwell world-wide fame.

Orwell suffered from tuberculosis and was in and out of hospital from 1947 until his death in 1950 at the age of forty-six.

All Orwell's works have been published in Penguins.

The following biographical note, probably written by Orwell himself, appeared on the jacket of the original edition of The Lion and the Unicorn:

'George Orwell was born in 1903 into an Anglo-Indian family and has had a varied history. He was a scholar of Eton, served five years in the Imperial Police in Burma, has been a dishwasher, a schoolmaster, and a bookseller's assistant, and fought and was wounded in the Spanish Civil War.

Best known among his books is *The Road to Wigan Pier*, with its unforgettable picture of the coalmining industry and the miseries of the Northern slums. Less widely read, but equally worthy of attention, are *Homage to Catalonia*, one of the best of the Spanish war books, and *Burmese Days*, one of the few outstanding novels of Anglo-Indian life.

Rejected by the Army on medical grounds, George Orwell is at present a film critic, book-reviewer and sergeant in the Home Guard.'

GEORGE ORWELL

The Lion and the Unicorn

Socialism and the English Genius

with an Introduction by Bernard Crick

Penguin Books

Penguin Books Ltd, Harmondsworth, Middlesex, England
Viking Penguin Inc., 40 West 23rd Street, New York, New York 10010, U.S.A.
Penguin Books Australia Ltd, Ringwood, Victoria, Australia
Penguin Books Canada Limited, 2801 John Street, Markham, Ontario, Canada L3R 1B4
Penguin Books (N.Z.) Ltd, 182 190 Wairau Road, Auckland 10, New Zealand

First published in the Searchlight Books series by Secker & Warburg 1941

Published in Volume 2 of *The Collected Essays, Journalism and Letters of George Orwell*
by Secker & Warburg 1968 and in Penguin Books 1970

Published separately with a new Introduction in Penguin Books 1982
Reprinted 1984, 1986

Copyright George Orwell, 1941
Introduction copyright © Bernard Crick, 1982
All rights reserved

Made and printed in Great Britain by
Richard Clay (The Chaucer Press) Ltd,
Bungay, Suffolk
Set in Monophoto Ehrhardt

Except in the United States of America, this book is sold subject
to the condition that it shall not, by way of trade or otherwise, be lent,
re-sold, hired out, or otherwise circulated without the
publisher's prior consent in any form of binding or cover other than
that in which it is published and without a similar condition
including this condition being imposed on the subsequent purchaser

CONTENTS

Introduction by Bernard Crick 7

THE LION AND THE UNICORN 31

PART ONE: England Your England 33

PART TWO: Shopkeepers at War 71

PART THREE: The English Revolution 93

INTRODUCTION

In an obituary notice in the *Observer* of 29 January 1950, Arthur Koestler wrote:

Among all the pamphlets, tracts and exhortations which the war produced, hardly anything bears re-reading today – except, perhaps, E. M. Forster's *What I Believe*, a few passages from Churchill's speeches, and, above all, Orwell's *The Lion and the Unicorn*. Its opening section, 'England Your England', is one of the most moving and yet incisive portraits of the English character, and a minor classic in itself.

And yet it is the least known of all his books. Until now it has been most readily accessible in, but also somewhat buried amidst, the second of the four volumes of the *Collected Essays*.[1] Rarely has it been considered on its own, as one of Orwell's most characteristic, stimulating and lively books and also as an important and characteristic writing in the tradition of 'English socialism', a work that sums up the thinking of the *Tribune* 'Old Left' as eloquently and persuasively as Michael Foot's life of Aneurin Bevan.

---

1. *The Collected Essays, Journalism and Letters of George Orwell*, ed. Sonia Orwell and Ian Angus, 4 vols. (Secker & Warburg, 1968; Penguin, 1970).

8 Introduction

There are, nonetheless, reasons for its neglect: the revolutionary Orwell revealed is not the Orwell that most people have been brought up on – that is, the gentle, liberal Orwell of the essays against censorship or the totally pessimistic or Cold War Orwell of the common misreading of *Nineteen Eighty-Four*.[2] And yet the revolutionary Orwell is revealed as not merely not a Marxist, but as positively a patriot, so he does not fit in with the expectations of contemporary advanced socialists either. What does not fit our expectations we commonly ignore or play down. But *The Lion and the Unicorn* is his fullest political statement: the values in it are those that *Nineteen Eighty-Four* warns us we could lose, and it is written in basically the same mood and mental framework as his next work, *Animal Farm* – the allegory of revolution betrayed, not of its impossibility. The style of *The Lion and the Unicorn* is vintage Orwell and he never changed – contrary to legend – the values expressed in it, neither his belief in the innate decency of ordinary people nor his belief in the growth of socialist values. All that happened was that after the end of the war (when the socialist revolution he foretold did not occur, only the coming of Clement Attlee as Prime Minister) he came to feel that the common values were as much threatened by ourselves as they had been by Hitler, and that specifically socialist values would take far longer to become generally held than he had hoped in 1941. In 1941 he plainly hoped to see 'the Republic' in his lifetime; by 1945 he had gained a more sad, realistic sense of time-scales, but he had not changed his values.

The Lion and the Unicorn does, however, contain some wild

2. As I sought to show in the last chapter of my *George Orwell: A Life* (Penguin, 1982), particularly to dispel the myth that it was his 'last testament' rather than the last book the poor fellow happened to have written before he happened to die.

political judgements. It was written quickly for a particular purpose and at that extraordinary time of great threat when Great Britain stood alone after the fall of France and before the Nazi invasion of Russia. The book is in one sense still very close to us, but in some other senses very remote. The context must be understood. And Orwell had taken a long time to come to both his famous plain style and his final moralistic socialism. We must be aware how long a journey it was, or else we read his earlier works with the misleading hindsight that comes from the common experience of reading his last two works first. Thus there is need now to say something about, first, the author; second, the circumstances of the commissioning of the book and its context; third, its structure and argument; and fourth, its achievement.

The Author

Orwell's background gave him an unusual perspective on the nature of Englishness or 'the English genius' of the subtitle. (It is, by the way, specifically the English of which he writes: he ignores Scotland, Wales and even Northern Ireland; he even shows deplorable anti-Scottish and anti-Irish prejudices; and a general fault of his argument is that he fails to consider how much the English character has been shaped by the multi-national culture and politics of the United Kingdom.) He was born in India but came to England when very young, was viciously and successfully crammed for Eton at a Prep school on a partial scholarship, but then rested on his oars at Eton – 'teach me if you can', as it were – although he read widely off the syllabus in his leisure. He claimed that his family were among the 'lower-upper-middle class', who were the upper-middle class without money. Lack both of that commodity and of examination results meant that he did not go to university but drifted in his father's footsteps into a minor and unfashionable branch of the Imperial Civil Service, though in his case the Burma Police, not the Indian Opium Service. He resigned after five years, coming to hate the British in Burma; and then for about eight years he lived the life of a poor and unsuccessful young writer. His first two novels, *Burmese Days* and *A Clergyman's Daughter*, were not published until 1935, but in 1933 Victor Gollancz had published his *Down and Out in Paris and London*, a slightly fictionalized account of two rather different experiences: living poor and rough in Paris after his money ran out and his manuscripts had been rejected, and deliberately living with tramps in England. He had disguised himself and lived, sometimes for weeks at a time, among tramps in order to see how the oppressed of his own country lived. This guilt-ridden and almost masochistic curiosity stemmed from his Burmese days. He was indeed a writer who, as V. S. Pritchett was to say, '"went native" in his own country'. *Burmese Days* was violently anti-imperialistic, just as *Down and Out* radiates a sympathy for the underdog; yet his reaction was complex and original: in neither case did he romanticize 'the natives', the victims of the system. However, neither attitude was by itself socialist. Orwell was perfectly familiar with socialist arguments, sometimes used them even before 1936, but he was not then a committed socialist and it is hindsight to read these early books in that way. When other young writers asked around 1930, 'Where do you stand?', he would reply that he was 'a Tory anarchist'.

'Tory anarchist' was not just jokey. He was an individualist who resented one man or one culture imposing its values on another, and above all resented servants of the state moralizing their power with talk of 'responsibility'. Tramps were tramps and always would be, the Burmans and others were in the power of Europeans, but that was no excuse for imposing one's own culture on them, in fact treating them like dirt. As late as 1935, his novel *Keep the Aspidistra Flying* shows no clear socialism, only the rage of the angry young man at how badly the 'money god' treats the artist and how commercial values degrade him into compromise. Only when Gollancz commissioned Orwell to go North and write a book about how the unemployed lived did it become clear (in *The Road to Wigan Pier* of 1937) that Orwell had committed himself to socialism. Typically, he did not put up at the local station hotel, nor for long in the clean and decent ordinary miner's house offered him, but at the filthiest place he could find, the famous tripe shop. Equally typically, part of *The Road to Wigan Pier* was a criticism of the failure of intellectual socialists to reach the common man, voiced at the very moment when he first announced his own socialism. But he had long kept company with 'advanced' socialists (indeed hardly with any 'ordinary' ones), knowing I.L.P.ers, Trotskyites and Communists well. Similarly, when he went to Spain later in 1936 he went to fight, not to write, and ended up not in the orthodox Communist-led International Brigade, but with the P.O.U.M., an independent Marxist party then strong in Catalonia which could best be described as Trotskyite if their leader had not quarrelled with Trotsky. Badly wounded, he returned to join the I.L.P., then far to the left of the Labour Party and strongly opposed to 'the coming capitalist war', and to denounce in *Homage to Catalonia* the Communist Party's suppression, as he argued, of the genuine revolution in Catalonia. He said that he had actually experienced socialism among the 'free Marxists' and the Anarchists in Catalonia. The socialist camp had gained an extraordinarily critical and independent member.

His next novel (and possibly his best), *Coming Up for Air*, shows a warm love of a traditional England of the 1900s that is being gradually destroyed by urban development and will shortly be utterly destroyed by a meaningless war. Some of his positive values – love of nature and of common sense, and an almost pietistic identification with common things – emerge through the eyes of an inadequate, excessively nostalgic, though beautifully portrayed, lower-middle-class anti-hero – though perhaps with a slight hint that his kind of people, if anyone, might one day (like the proles in *Nineteen Eighty-Four*) be able to do better, or, rather, get back on to a lost path before trying to move forward again. And on the very eve of war, in July 1939, the month after the novel appeared, came an article, 'Not Counting Niggers', which violently mocked the anti-fascist alliance of 'Quakers shouting for a bigger army, Communists waving union jacks, Winston Churchill posing as a democrat'. Schemes for the democracies to stand together against the dictatorships always ignored, he argued, 'six hundred million disenfranchised human beings', the 'niggers'. The so-called democracies were 'in essence nothing but mechanisms for exploiting cheap labour'. He ended:

Nothing is likely to save us except the emergence within the next two years of a real mass party whose first pledges are to refuse war and to right imperial injustice. But if any such party exists at present, it is only as a possibility, in a few tiny germs lying here and there in unwatered soil.[3]

Such was Orwell's position scarcely eighteen months before he began to write *The Lion and the Unicorn*. When war did break out he at once came to see that there was 'no real alternative between resisting Hitler and surrendering to him',

3. *Collected Essays*, Vol. 1, no. 155.

and that surrender would 'make nonsense of the Republican resistance in Spain, the Chinese resistance to Japan, etc. etc.'. And he admitted in an essay of 1940 that it was not just a case of defending the bad against the worse, but that he felt a positive surge of patriotism: 'that long drilling which the middle classes go through had done its work'. But, surprisingly, he then briskly synthesized pre-war revolutionary fervour and his newly regained patriotism – and this was the mental birth of *The Lion and the Unicorn*:

> ... let no one mistake the meaning of this. Patriotism has nothing to do with conservatism. It is devotion to something that is changing but is felt to be mystically the same ... To be loyal both to Chamberlain's England and to the England of tomorrow might seem an impossibility, if one did not know it to be an everyday phenomenon. Only revolution can save England, that has been obvious for years, but now the revolution has started and it may proceed quite quickly if only we can keep Hitler out. Within two years, maybe a year, if only we can hang on, we shall see changes that will surprise the idiots who have no foresight. I dare say the London gutters will have to run with blood. All right, let them, if it is necessary. But when the red militias are billeted in the Ritz I shall still feel that the England I was taught to love so long ago and for such different reasons is somehow persisting.[4]

He said that he had come to this position just before the actual outbreak of war: that the night before the Hitler–Stalin pact was signed he had had a dream that war had broken out, and that from this dream he had realized the true state of his feelings. Indeed that same Hitler–Stalin pact of 1939, which drove many fellow-travellers away from the Communist Party, strengthened a belief that had been growing in Orwell's mind since Spain that Stalinism and Nazism had, for all their antagonism, many things in common: that they deserved the

4. *Collected Essays*, Vol. 1, no. 168.

new appellation 'totalitarian'. This emerged in his essay on 'Fascism and Democracy' in Victor Gollancz's symposium of March 1941, *The Betrayal of the Left: An Examination and Refutation of Communist Policy*, and more fully in his essay 'Wells, Hitler and the World State' of the following year. But neither his adoption of the totalitarian hypothesis nor his falling in behind the war effort affected his left-wing socialism, so bitingly libertarian but also stridently egalitarian – as is demonstrated by his second contribution to *The Betrayal of the Left*, 'Patriots and Revolutionaries', an essay that also covered some of the same ground as *The Lion and the Unicorn*.[5]

This militant phase of Orwell's, from 1937 to about 1944, is under-represented in the *Collected Essays*, so that *The Lion and the Unicorn* appears as a somewhat eccentric piece of 'one-off' writing amid wider literary concerns, rather than something central to his thoughts. With Orwell it was always a matter of balance; liberty and equality were companions, not antagonists: even in his most politically active phase he defended as pure literature the work of a writer like Henry Miller whose social prejudices he detested; and even in his post-war seclusion on the island of Jura, and during those long months of fighting tuberculosis in sanatoria and hospitals, his socialism still burned strong, if not quite with the wildfire of 1940.

Orwell tried hard to enlist in the army but his lungs let him down, though he thought that the War Office discriminated against those who had fought for the Republic in Spain. He eventually got a job with the BBC, which he disliked and soon left to become – probably in part as a result of writing *The Lion and the Unicorn* – literary editor of *Tribune*. The

---

5. Neither of these essays are included in the *Collected Essays*, but Secker & Warburg have now commissioned Mr Ian Angus to revise the *Collected Essays* and to add an additional volume of the rest of Orwell's published writings.

closest he got to the main war effort was joining the Home Guard, in which he was an effective but unorthodox platoon sergeant. And he actually believed, during the time he was writing this book, that the Home Guard should and could become a revolutionary popular army. This belief was eccentric, but he wrote notes for lectures on guerrilla warfare and on the need for popular political aims to influence military tactics and strategy which were far in advance of most military thinking of the day.

The Commissioning of the Book

Tosco Fyvel was introduced to Orwell by Fredric Warburg (of Secker & Warburg), who had published his *No Ease in Zion* and Orwell's *Homage to Catalonia*. During the 1930s Fyvel had worked in Palestine for Golda Meir in the trade union organization. He was there at the time of the Arab Rebellion of 1936 and had met Orde Wingate, a man with a genius for the tactics of irregular warfare as well as a Protestant fundamentalist sympathy with Zionism. Wingate urged Fyvel to return to Great Britain for the war, to spread his doctrine of the overriding importance of war aims, the primacy of the political over the military and the superiority of the citizen-soldier over the professional. As often with great and unwelcome new ideas, nothing more and nothing less than a new publishing series resulted. Warburg, Fyvel, Orwell and Sebastian Haffner (a German refugee, later German correspondent of the *Observer*) formed a small 'war aims' committee, discussing who should say what in 'an important new series'.

The 'Publisher's Announcement' proclaimed:

Nazism has plotted and organized for twenty years... We cannot defeat Germany until we have first freed ourselves from our own weaknesses. It is the aim of SEARCHLIGHT BOOKS to do all in their power to criticize and kill what is rotten in Western civilization and supply constructive ideas for the difficult period ahead of us. The series ... will stress Britain's international and imperial responsibilities at the head of a greater and freer British Commonwealth, linked with the United States of America and other countries, as a framework of world order. The books will be written in simple language without the rubber-stamp political jargon of the past. They will seek to appeal to the new generation which is fighting this war whether on the battlefields or in the factories and to all those who can recognize the spirit of the new world ...

Orwell's hand is obvious. And Fyvel persuaded a somewhat reluctant Orwell to write for the series himself. Putting so much energy into trying to enlist or to get a 'real' job to help the war effort, Orwell had given up 'trying to write', meaning novels, although as ever he was writing lots of book reviews and occasional pieces (even letters to *Time and Tide* urging 'Arm the People!' and articles in *Tribune* urging left-wing socialists to join the Home Guard and get a gun). So perhaps he welcomed the chance to write a long pamphlet or a short book that would pull together and extend several themes he had floated in occasional pieces. He wrote it in London during the worst time of the blitz, working at it off and on between August and October 1940. It was published on 19 February 1941, and was the first volume in the new series.

The other books in the series were really long pamphlets, all priced at two shillings. Orwell worked hard with Fyvel at finding authors and reading manuscripts. They worked up a good list together. The published books were, in addition to Orwell's, Sebastian Haffner, *Offensive Against Germany*; Ritchie Calder, *The Lesson of London*; 'Cassandra', *The English at*

War; T. C. Worsley, *The End of 'The Old School Tie'*; Arturo Barea, *The Struggle for the Spanish Soul*; Joyce Cary, *The Case for African Freedom*; B. Causton, *The Moral Blitz: War Propaganda and Christianity*; Olaf Stapledon, *Beyond the 'Isms'*; and Stephen Spender, *Life and the Poet*. And books had been commissioned from Michael Foot, Cyril Connolly, Tosco Fyvel, George Catlin, Arthur Koestler and François Lafitte before the series came to an abrupt end early in 1942 when Secker & Warburg's printers at Portsmouth were bombed, destroying most of their stock and all of their paper. The Orwell had sold about ten thousand copies before the disaster, second only to Cassandra's sales, a good number for the conditions. With paper rationing, new books, particularly topical ones, were passed from hand to hand, so Fred Warburg reckoned that at least 50,000 people must have read it. Thus it was much the most widely read of Orwell's books (except possibly the Left Book Club edition of *The Road to Wigan Pier*) before *Animal Farm*.

Structure and Argument

The book falls into three parts: 'England Your England' is about the national character; 'Shopkeepers at War' is about socialism and the class system; and 'The English Revolution' is simply about the peculiarly English form the revolution will take, while being a revolution nonetheless.

'National character' is a concept that most social scientists and historians try hard to avoid, but without which one cannot understand the real world. If 'fools rush in where angels fear to tread', Orwell is at least a wise fool. There are few other such essays on the English character worth reading; this is not to say that the celebratory offerings of Sir Arthur Bryant and

Dr A. L. Rowse are not well written, but they are simply not critical. Orwell has an extraordinary critical empathy: he stands within the family but is able both to praise it and to blame it strongly, standing both close and far. His biography may help to explain his critical distancing, but unlike so many left-wing intellectuals, he was not merely critical. He loved his native land for all its faults. Indeed the red thread of argument running through all three sections of the book is that the Left has as great a claim to patriotism as the Right, and is at its strongest when it takes radical traditions as the starting point for revolutionary change.

England, he said, was 'a family with the wrong members in control'. Some socialist critics of Orwell see this metaphor as selling the pass: it hardly matters who is in control, it is the assumption of there being a family at all that is wrong and quietistic: the reality is class war. But Orwell stubbornly insists, polemically delighting to rub his own cat's fur the wrong way, that national character is inescapable: even socialists cannot by act of will become cosmopolitan or free-floating intellectuals. And if one looks at the contradictory characteristics of Englishness, one can see good things to be built upon and bad things to be torn down. But only if one recognizes the force of patriotism can one hope to control it for egalitarian and libertarian ends.

The first section, 'England Your England', argues that 'the gentleness of English civilization is perhaps its most marked characteristic ... It is a land where the bus conductors are good-tempered and the police carry no revolvers.' But it is also 'the most class-ridden country under the sun ... ruled largely by the old and silly'. He argued that it would be better for ordinary working people (who have more common sense, morality, decency and sociability than their rulers) if they had more confidence in their ability to manage the affairs of the family for themselves; and better for socialist intellectuals to give up vague talk of 'new values' for a 'new age' and to look under their noses at the actual values held by the common people. After all, it is their land; they work it with their hands. Now Orwell showed considerable historical sense in realizing that the very concept of 'patriotism' in England had radical roots: 'our country' because we work it with our hands – this had been a rallying cry of seventeenth- and eighteenth-century radicals. They regarded the aristocracy as tainted with cosmopolitanism, and it took a very long time for the House of Hanover to be transmuted but not fully muted into the House of Windsor. When Dr Johnson roared out, 'Patriotism, Sir, is the last refuge of a scoundrel', he was not reneging on his own Toryism, he was sounding off against 'that devil Wilkes', whose followers called themselves 'the patriots' in imitation of the American radicals who, in turn, took it from the whole republican tradition, partly mythological and partly historical.

Now 'gentleness' and 'toleration' are good characteristics to Orwell, though no one was more aware that to defend them one cannot always, in every circumstance, be gentle or tolerant. And not for one moment did Orwell assume that English patriotism was better than other people's. Each tradition must be examined on its own. We apply general standards of judgement, but conditions vary. All he insists upon is that we cannot ever fully escape national traditions, nor should we try; that indeed the Left would be stronger and carry more conviction if it could embrace the intense patriotism, love of country, love of local oddities, of the old radical movement, rather than the new pseudo-cosmopolitanism of the Marxists. Nor did he deny the importance of class structure and domination; indeed much of the book is about just this. But he did deny that class is the only conditioning factor, which shows how his untheoretical mind could produce a more profound observation than the vulgar Marxism of his day was capable of. 'Patriotism takes different forms in different classes,' he wrote, 'but it runs like a connecting thread through nearly all of them.' He had rude doubts about the upper classes.[6]

The second section, 'Shopkeepers at War', argues that 'the war has demonstrated that private capitalism ... *does not work*', and that 'it is only by revolution that the English people can be set free'. But revolution to Orwell is not a *coup d'état*, it is a mass movement: if there are sudden bloody events, it will be through counter-revolution when the expropriators refuse to be expropriated. This was in fact a characteristic argument of English left-wing socialists. 'Revolution' was to be seen as a process and not as an event; it need not be violent to break up the old class structure, but it could have violence thrust upon it by resistance to socialist Parliamentary legislation. (Harold Laski lost a famous libel action on the narrow distinction between advocating violent revolution, which he had been reported as doing, and warning that socialist legislation would provoke a revolutionary situation, though triggered by 'sabotage' from the Right.)

Yet precisely because a revolution for freedom and equality must be a voluntary mass movement, 'the shopkeepers' need to be persuaded. Just as in the second part of *The Road to Wigan Pier*, Orwell argues that it is a typical vice of the Labour movement to talk to itself. He might still have held such a view today. Socialists need to persuade others: hence the importance of patriotism and the war as a demonstration

6. He went over the same ground as 'England Your England' once again, virtually rewriting the same material, though with the politics toned down, as a 'wretched potboiler', he said, for a Collins 'Britain in Pictures' series: George Orwell, *The English People* (Collins, 1946). As usual, his self-deprecation was exaggerated.

that planned economies can work and that the capitalist system has failed. He attaches great importance to something that had never existed before 1918:

... people of indeterminate social class. In 1910 every human being in these islands could be 'placed' in an instant by his clothes, manners and accent. That is no longer the case. Above all it is not the case in the new townships that have developed as a result of cheap motor-cars and the southward shift of industry. The place to look for the terms of the future England is in light-industry areas and along the arterial roads ... To that civilization belong the people who are most at home in and most definitely *of* the modern world, the technicians and the higher paid skilled workers, the airmen and the mechanics, the radio experts, film producers, popular journalists and industrial chemists. They are the indeterminate stratum at which the older class distinctions are beginning to break down.

Had he lived, he might have added social workers and polytechnic lecturers to his list. Elsewhere he talks of the 'lower-middle class' as having the same role: a leadership role. Orwell is at least original in arguing that leadership for the working class is likely to emerge neither from among themselves nor from the intelligentsia (still less from left-wing politicians posing as working class), but from the 'indeterminate stratum' or the old lower-middle class. The object of socialist propaganda must be to win these people over.

Yet he is careful, even before James Burnham and Milovan Djilas, to warn against the emergence of a new class of public service bureaucrats – such as he satirized as 'the Party' in *Nineteen Eighty-Four*:

Centralized ownership has very little meaning unless the mass of the people are living roughly upon an equal level, and have some kind of control over the government. 'The State' may come to mean no more than a self-elected political party, and oligarchy and privilege can return, based on power rather than on money.

For a 'non-theorist' Orwell hits on some remarkably important theses remarkably early. And he is among the first to have grasped that 'War is the greatest of all agents of change. It speeds up all processes, wipes out minor distinctions, brings reality to the surface. Above all it brings home to the individual that he is *not* altogether an individual.' This is brave as well as original thinking, for most left-wing intellectuals would dismiss any historical speculation of this kind as Nietzschean romanticism, or suspect Orwell of justifying war rather than simply understanding unexpected social consequences and opportunities – although Trotsky had once said that 'war is the locomotive of social change'. But notice too his remark about individualism: war does indeed create a consciousness of fraternity.

The third section, 'The English Revolution', argues that 'the English revolution' is under way, especially in the ranks of the army, and that: 'The war and the revolution are inseparable. We cannot establish anything that a Western nation would regard as Socialism without defeating Hitler; on the other hand we cannot defeat Hitler while we remain economically and socially in the nineteenth century.' Alas (or 'thank god', some might say) it was all a wild exaggeration of social trends that did lead to inescapable political demands for post-war reconstruction, forcing the Beveridge Report out of Churchill's Coalition Government and leading to the Labour victory of 1945. But none of this could reasonably be called revolutionary, except in gentler senses than Orwell appears to mean. In a sense it was revolutionary for both parties to accept the need for full employment and a Welfare State, but this left the class system largely untouched, in some ways protected it; and certainly it did not take, thirty-four years later, a revolution to begin turning the clock back even on that advance, only a close election result following a change of power within the Conservative Party. If he exaggerated wildly, he did have a sense that something fundamental was happening which went far deeper than the utilitarian need to pay some attention to the home front as part of war strategy. And it is endlessly arguable whether the ferment in public opinion during the war, the vague but passionate desire to break from the past, could not have resulted in something at least more self-consciously revolutionary than came from Clement Attlee's regime. It took Conservatives some time to realize that the revolution was not taking place, that Attlee and Morrison were at the helm, not Cripps and Bevan. Orwell's hopes seemed to mirror Tory fears. He made the same mistake as when he once said that the Peace Pledge Union was a product of the Navy League – that is, that extremists tend to feed off each other. His judgements were wrong, but simply to apply hindsight and dismiss them as silly is to accept that everything that has happened must have happened, and, empirically, is to underestimate the tremendous social and political ferment, the sense both of uncertainty and of changing possibilities, of the wartime years. If the Labour Party was ever to have acted as a socialist party (and Orwell makes clear that he regarded it as basically a trade-union party, though for want of anything better he now supported it with a very qualified loyalty), perhaps 1945, not 1964, was its historic lost opportunity.

There are, however, three features of this section whose importance is unaffected by Orwell's over-optimism. The first is the actual six-point programme he advocated (see p. 104). For all its vagueness, it was very much the kind of programme that the *Tribune* group and later the Bevanites espoused. There is no essential mystery about Orwell's politics after he left the I.L.P. in 1939 when Fenner Brockway and others opposed the war: he was a '*Tribune* socialist', and such he remained until his death. The idea that he changed his politics, renounced his socialism (as 'proved' by *Nineteen Eighty-Four*), is pure myth, sometimes arising from pure muddle, but sometimes deliberately fostered by people who like his anti-Communism and his defence of free expression, clear expression and literary values, but cannot stomach his rabid egalitarianism. Such people normally ignore *The Lion and the Unicorn*, or imply that he must have been especially ill or momentarily dotty when he wrote it. It is odd that people admire Orwell's practice and defence of plain English style so much, while ignoring much of the content of what he said about English society and English character. By 1950 Arthur Koestler no longer shared Orwell's politics except in exposing the pretension of the Russian Government to be socialist; but he nonetheless drew attention to this book's importance and neglect among Orwell's writings.

The second important feature of this third section is that it reveals Orwell's political thought as by no means typically liberal, but standing rather in a harsher, more realistic republican tradition, partly Jacobinical, partly old English Puritan. Liberty is not just being left alone, it is up and doing: a positive freedom of active citizenry. In a remarkable paragraph he describes what his hoped-for English revolution will do, so undoctrinaire and so illogical, leaving loose ends everywhere and maintaining many odd traditions, like the 'ridiculous horsehair wig' of the judges and 'the lion and the unicorn on the soldier's cap-buttons' (see p. 113). Nonetheless, 'it will have nationalized industry, scaled down incomes, set up a classless educational system', all of which is 'the essential thing' and enough to stir violent opposition:

It will shoot traitors, but it will give them a solemn trial beforehand and occasionally it will acquit them. It will crush any open revolt promptly and cruelly, but it will interfere very little with the spoken and written word.

Is this foolish posturing, playing at being Danton in the June Days, or a Roman republican? But the history of Europe might have been better and different if the Weimar Republic had defended itself in that republican spirit instead of, like the good liberal, respecting the rule of law until it was too late. This is not the place to argue the merits of these two traditions, but simply to indicate in which of them Orwell stood. No 'proto-Social Democrat' he.

The third important point is embedded in this same passage. He argues that the English revolution 'will show a power of assimilating the past which will shock foreign observers and sometimes make them doubt whether any revolution has happened'. Why this must be so becomes a little more clear in the last paragraph of the book:

The heirs of Nelson and Cromwell are not in the House of Lords. They are in the fields and the streets, in the factories and the armed forces, in the four-ale bar and the suburban back garden; and at present they are kept under by a generation of ghosts. Compared with the task of bringing the real England to the surface, even the winning of the war, necessary though it is, is secondary. By revolution we become more ourselves, not less.

Orwell genuinely believed, no mere platitude or rhetoric this, in the innate 'decency' (the word he is fond of) of ordinary people. True values are not to be created nor old values 'transfigured' by the revolution, or in a new revolutionary consciousness; they exist already in the decency, fraternity, mutual aid, sociability, tolerance and scepticism towards authority of the working class – values which have survived the competitive individualism and reduction of everything to money values, engendered by capitalism, which has almost swallowed the middle classes. They need but to be brought to the surface, to come up for air. The oppressed have been less corrupted than the oppressors: a view presented again in *Nineteen Eighty-Four*, where remains of genuine humanity, compassion and fellow feeling, indeed flickers of a true memory of the past, are to be found among the Proles, not among the party elite: 'The Proles had stayed human. They had not become hardened inside. They had held on to primitive emotions which he himself had to re-learn by conscious effort.'

Whether or not he romanticizes or exaggerates, this is his view. 'Decency' is not an empty word, but is part of the moral values of socialism which are embedded in working-class culture.[7] He was perfectly aware of how Marxist theory reduced all values to mere instruments of class oppression or reflections of a particular mode of production, and he rejected this theory. He does not waste time here mocking its abstract rigidity (though he did in *The Road to Wigan Pier*); he simply states the alternative in homely, simple, publicly understandable terms. Socialism must relate to a specific historical consciousness, argues Orwell. The general principles of liberty, equality, fraternity and social justice must emerge from particular national traditions, specifically those of the working classes in each nation: they are not something to be

7. As Richard Taylor shows in a most interesting essay, 'George Orwell and the Politics of Decency', in *George Orwell*, Bradford Centre Occasional Paper No. 3 (University of Leeds Department of Adult Education, October 1981).

thrust upon them for their own good. And Orwell held to the unusual view that socialists have a peculiar duty to write about theories, values and policies in a way comprehensible to ordinary literate people (unlike much contemporary socialist writing, of his generation and ours). Style, meaning and audience must all go together.

The Achievement

By the standard of writing that Orwell set for himself in his essay of 1946, 'Why I Write', *The Lion and the Unicorn* at least partially succeeds, and has more literary merit than at least two of his novels:

> What I have most wanted to do in the past ten years is to make political writing into an art ... looking back through my work, I see that it is invariably where I lacked a *political* purpose that I wrote lifeless books and was betrayed into purple passages, sentences without meaning, decorative adjectives and humbug generally.

I think 'partially succeeds' because Orwell claimed in the same essay that '*Animal Farm* was the first book in which I tried, with full consciousness of what I was doing, to fuse political purpose and artistic purpose into one whole' – and how greatly he succeeded. *The Lion and the Unicorn* obviously had no equivalent to the artistic purpose of *Animal Farm*: to find the simplest possible form of allegory and story – a 'Fairy Story' indeed, as the subtitle states.

The Lion and the Unicorn is a marvellous piece of polemical prose, as good as anything in the collection of British pamphleteers which he jointly edited.[8] But it has to be judged as a

8. George Orwell and Reginald Reynolds (eds.), *British Pamphleteers*, Vol. 1 (Wingate, 1948).

pamphlet. If the 'artistic purpose' is limited and straightforward, still the 'political purpose' rarely has room for dispassionate analysis or time for philosophical justification of an argument.

V. S. Pritchett saw it all in his lead review in the *New Statesman and Nation* (1 March 1941):

Mr George Orwell has many of the traits of the best English pamphleteers: courage, an individual mind, vehement opinions, an instinct for stirring up trouble, the arts of appealing to that imaginary creature the sensible man and of combining original observations with sweeping generalization, of seeing enemies everywhere and despising all of them. And like the two outstanding figures of our tradition of pamphleteering, Cobbett and Defoe, both of whom had his subversive, non-conforming brand of patriotism, he writes a lucid conversational style which wakes one up suddenly like cold water dashed in the face. The sting of it is sometimes refreshing; sometimes it makes one very angry. For Mr Orwell likes his friends no better than his enemies and in the name of common sense is capable of exaggerating with the simplicity and innocence of a savage. His virtue is that he says things that need to be said; his vice that some of those things needed saying with a great deal more consideration.

That is the difficulty. Pamphlets tend to exaggeration, so it is some of the political judgements of *The Lion and the Unicorn*, rather than the form and style, that flaw the achievement. The polemic insists that a revolution is coming, is indeed already under way; but this tends to obscure the important, cooler and more analytical judgements about the nature of English society and tempts him into challenging, interesting assertions such as those about the precise nature of working-class moral beliefs that cry out, indeed, for 'more consideration'. And he offers few rigorous justifications for policies he advocates, only appeals to common sense; his presuppositions have to be dug for, although they can usually be found.

If Orwell's political thought is hardly systematic, it is nonetheless brilliantly expressive of that tradition of 'English socialism' which, through William Morris, Robert Blatchford, Edward Carpenter, the early H. G. Wells, R. H. Tawney, G. D. H. Cole, Harold Laski and Aneurin Bevan, has argued that only in a radically more egalitarian, more fraternal and less competitive society can liberties flourish and abound for all and ordinary people thus achieve their full human potential. It has been a tradition that has stressed the importance of ethical commitment, social justice and personal example, and has believed more (though it can be a matter of relative emphasis rather than absolute dichotomy) in the possibility and importance of freely held values than in the systematic theories of continental socialism and Marxism, which stress structural factors of class or modes of production.

Indeed, not merely is *The Lion and the Unicorn* expressive of 'English socialism', it is almost the last popular statement of it with any literary merit written in a way that ordinary people, with only secondary education, could comprehend. It is hard to think of any subsequent socialist books that have not been uncompromisingly academic or theoretical in their language; or else, if occasionally written for a wider audience, without neologistic jargon, have not proved to be ephemeral polemics. The post-war world, for all the massive increase in educational provision, has been dominated by mass media which reach 'the people', indeed, but which can only think short-term, and trivialize, sensationalize and entertain, consciously or unconsciously working against political understanding, against the development of a politically literate and active majority. All this Orwell viciously satirized as 'prolecult' in *Nineteen Eighty-Four*, not as something new in the future but as something with us already. *The Lion and the Unicorn* has its faults, but it is both profound and popular and of lasting value.

How Orwell wished the book to be read can seen from the text of the 1941 dust jacket:

This original book is a study of England and of England's special problems in an age when private capitalism is dissolving into a classless, ownerless society.

Cutting across the ordinary classifications, it insists that England, like all great countries, has its own peculiar destiny, and that the imitation of foreign political methods and habits of thought has been a disastrous error. Against the conventional patriots it urges the impossibility of winning the war without far-reaching social reconstruction; against the conventional left-wingers it urges the uselessness of aiming at any version of Socialism that does not take account of English history and character. It sets out, in its own words, to reconcile patriotism with intelligence.

The first part of the book is a study of the social atmosphere of England and an attempt to determine just how much reality, and how much humbug, British democracy contains. The second part emphasizes the disastrous effects of social injustice on a nation engaged in total war. The third part sets forth a simple concrete policy of a kind that the English people might be induced to follow. This is a book for those who are neither ashamed of being Englishmen nor satisfied with England as it now is.[9]

9. I thank the Rt Hon. Kenneth Baker, M.P. (as book-collector, not as a Government Minister), for finding me this dust-jacket, a copy of which is not even in the Orwell Archive at University College, London.

*The Lion
and the Unicorn*

PART ONE:

England Your England

I

As I write, highly civilized human beings are flying overhead, trying to kill me.

They do not feel any enmity against me as an individual, nor I against them. They are 'only doing their duty', as the saying goes. Most of them, I have no doubt, are kind-hearted law-abiding men who would never dream of committing murder in private life. On the other hand, if one of them succeeds in blowing me to pieces with a well-placed bomb, he will never sleep any the worse for it. He is serving his country, which has the power to absolve him from evil.

One cannot see the modern world as it is unless one recognizes the overwhelming strength of patriotism, national loyalty. In certain circumstances it can break down, at certain levels of civilization it does not exist, but as a *positive* force there is nothing to set beside it. Christianity and international Socialism are as weak as straw in comparison with it. Hitler and Mussolini rose to power in their own countries very largely because they could grasp this fact and their opponents could not.

Also, one must admit that the divisions between nation and nation are founded on real differences of outlook. Till recently it was thought proper to pretend that all human beings are very much alike, but in fact anyone able to use his eyes knows that the average of human behaviour differs enormously from country to country. Things that could happen in one country could not happen in another. Hitler's June purge, for instance, could not have happened in England. And, as western peoples go, the English are very highly differentiated. There is a sort of back-handed admission of this in the dislike which nearly all foreigners feel for our national way of life. Few Europeans can endure living in England, and even Americans often feel more at home in Europe.

When you come back to England from any foreign country, you have immediately the sensation of breathing a different air. Even in the first few minutes dozens of small things conspire to give you this feeling. The beer is bitterer, the coins are heavier, the grass is greener, the advertisements are more blatant. The crowds in the big towns, with their mild knobby faces, their bad teeth and gentle manners, are different from a European crowd. Then the vastness of England swallows you up, and you lose for a while your feeling that the whole nation has a single identifiable character. Are there really such things as nations? Are we not forty-six million individuals, all different? And the diversity of it, the chaos! The clatter of clogs in the Lancashire mill towns, the to-and-fro of the lorries on the Great North Road, the queues outside the Labour Exchanges, the rattle of pintables in the Soho pubs, the old maids biking to Holy Communion through the mists of the autumn morning – all these are not only fragments, but *characteristic* fragments, of the English scene. How can one make a pattern out of this muddle?

But talk to foreigners, read foreign books or newspapers, and you are brought back to the same thought. Yes, there *is* something distinctive and recognizable in English civilization. It is a culture as individual as that of Spain. It is somehow bound up with solid breakfasts and gloomy Sundays, smoky towns and winding roads, green fields and red pillar-boxes. It has a flavour of its own. Moreover it is continuous, it stretches into the future and the past, there is something in it that persists, as in a living creature. What can the England of 1940 have in common with the England of 1840? But then, what have you in common with the child of five whose photograph your mother keeps on the mantelpiece? Nothing, except that you happen to be the same person.

And above all, it is *your* civilization, it is *you*. However much you hate it or laugh at it, you will never be happy away from it for any length of time. The suet puddings and the red pillar-boxes have entered into your soul. Good or evil, it is yours, you belong to it, and this side the grave you will never get away from the marks that it has given you.

Meanwhile England, together with the rest of the world, is changing. And like everything else it can change only in certain directions, which up to a point can be foreseen. That is not to say that the future is fixed, merely that certain alternatives are possible and others not. A seed may grow or not grow, but at any rate a turnip seed never grows into a parsnip. It is therefore of the deepest importance to try and determine what England *is*, before guessing what part England *can play* in the huge events that are happening.

II

National characteristics are not easy to pin down, and when pinned down they often turn out to be trivialities or seem to have no connexion with one another. Spaniards are cruel to animals, Italians can do nothing without making a deafening noise, the Chinese are addicted to gambling. Obviously such things don't matter in themselves. Nevertheless, nothing is causeless, and even the fact that Englishmen have bad teeth can tell something about the realities of English life.

Here are a couple of generalizations about England that would be accepted by almost all observers. One is that the English are not gifted artistically. They are not as musical as the Germans or Italians, painting and sculpture have never flourished in England as they have in France. Another is that, as Europeans go, the English are not intellectual. They have a horror of abstract thought, they feel no need for any philosophy or systematic 'world-view'. Nor is this because they are 'practical', as they are so fond of claiming for themselves. One has only to look at their methods of town planning and water supply, their obstinate clinging to everything that is out of date and a nuisance, a spelling system that defies analysis, and a system of weights and measures that is intelligible only to the compilers of arithmetic books, to see how little they care about mere efficiency. But they have a certain power of acting without taking thought. Their world-famed hypocrisy – their double-faced attitude towards the Empire, for instance – is bound up with this. Also, in moments of supreme crisis the whole nation can suddenly draw together and act upon a species of instinct, really a code of conduct which is understood by almost everyone, though never formulated. The phrase that Hitler coined for the Germans, 'a sleep-walking people', would have been better applied to the English. Not that there is anything to be proud of in being called a sleep-walker.

But here it is worth noting a minor English trait which is extremely well marked though not often commented on, and that is a love of flowers. This is one of the first things that one notices when one reaches England from abroad, especially if one is coming from southern Europe. Does it not contradict the English indifference to the arts? Not really, because it is found in people who have no aesthetic feelings whatever. What it does link up with, however, is another English characteristic which is so much a part of us that we barely notice it, and that is the addiction to hobbies and spare-time occupations, the *privateness* of English life. We are a nation of flower-lovers, but also a nation of stamp-collectors, pigeon-fanciers, amateur carpenters, coupon-snippers, darts-players, crossword-puzzle fans. All the culture that is most truly native centres round things which even when they are communal are not official – the pub, the football match, the back garden, the fireside and the 'nice cup of tea'. The liberty of the individual is still believed in, almost as in the nineteenth century. But this has nothing to do with economic liberty, the right to exploit others for profit. It is the liberty to have a home of your own, to do what you like in your spare time, to choose your own amusements instead of having them chosen for you from above. The most hateful of all names in an English ear is Nosey Parker. It is obvious, of course, that even this purely private liberty is a lost cause. Like all other modern people, the English are in process of being numbered, labelled, conscripted, 'co-ordinated'. But the pull of their impulses is in the other direction, and the kind of regimentation that can be imposed on them will be modified in consequence. No party rallies, no Youth Movements, no coloured shirts, no Jew-baiting or 'spontaneous' demonstrations. No Gestapo either, in all probability.

But in all societies the common people must live to some extent *against* the existing order. The genuinely popular culture of England is something that goes on beneath the surface, unofficially and more or less frowned on by the authorities. One thing one notices if one looks directly at the common people, especially in the big towns, is that they are not puritanical. They are inveterate gamblers, drink as much beer as their wages will permit, are devoted to bawdy jokes, and use probably the foulest language in the world. They have to satisfy these tastes in the face of astonishing, hypocritical laws (licensing laws, lottery acts, etc. etc.) which are designed to interfere with everybody but in practice allow everything to happen. Also, the common people are without definite religious belief, and have been so for centuries. The Anglican Church never had a real hold on them, it was simply a preserve of the landed gentry, and the Nonconformist sects only influenced minorities. And yet they have retained a deep tinge of Christian feeling, while almost forgetting the name of Christ.

The power-worship which is the new religion of Europe, and which has infected the English intelligentsia, has never touched the common people. They have never caught up with power politics. The 'realism' which is preached in Japanese and Italian newspapers would horrify them. One can learn a good deal about the spirit of England from the comic coloured postcards that you see in the windows of cheap stationers' shops. These things are a sort of diary upon which the English people have unconsciously recorded themselves. Their old-fashioned outlook, their graded snobberies, their mixture of bawdiness and hypocrisy, their extreme gentleness, their deeply moral attitude to life, are all mirrored there.

The gentleness of the English civilization is perhaps its most marked characteristic. You notice it the instant you set foot on English soil. It is a land where the bus conductors are good-tempered and the policemen carry no revolvers. In no country inhabited by white men is it easier to shove people off the pavement. And with this goes something that is always written off by European observers as 'decadence' or hypocrisy, the English hatred of war and militarism. It is rooted deep in history, and it is strong in the lower-middle class as well as the working class. Successive wars have shaken it but not destroyed it. Well within living memory it was common for 'the redcoats' to be booed at in the streets and for the landlords of respectable public houses to refuse to allow soldiers on the premises. In peace time, even when there are two million unemployed, it is difficult to fill the ranks of the tiny standing army, which is officered by the county gentry and a specialized stratum of the middle class, and manned by farm labourers and slum proletarians. The mass of the people are without military knowledge or tradition, and their attitude towards war is invariably defensive. No politician could rise to power by promising them conquests or military 'glory', no Hymn of Hate has ever made any appeal to them. In the last war the songs which the soldiers made up and sang of their own accord were not vengeful but humorous and mock-defeatist.[1] The only enemy they ever named was the sergeant-major.

In England all the boasting and flag-wagging, the 'Rule Britannia' stuff, is done by small minorities. The patriotism of the common people is not vocal or even conscious. They do not retain among their historical memories the name of a single military victory. English literature, like other literatures, is full of battle-poems, but it is worth noticing that the ones that have won for themselves a kind of popularity are always a tale of disasters and retreats. There is no popular poem about Trafalgar or Waterloo, for instance. Sir John Moore's army at Corunna, fighting a desperate rearguard action before escaping overseas (just like Dunkirk!) has more appeal than a brilliant victory. The most stirring battle-poem in English is about a brigade of cavalry which charged in the wrong direction. And of the last war, the four names which have really engraved themselves on the popular memory are Mons, Ypres, Gallipoli and Passchendaele, every time a disaster. The names of the great battles that finally broke the German armies are simply unknown to the general public.

The reason why the English anti-militarism disgusts foreign observers is that it ignores the existence of the British Empire. It looks like sheer hypocrisy. After all, the English have absorbed a quarter of the earth and held on to it by means of

1. For example:
>'I don't want to join the bloody Army,
>I don't want to go unto the war;
>I want no more to roam,
>I'd rather stay at home,
>Living on the earnings of a whore.'

But it was not in that spirit that they fought. [Author's footnote.]

a huge navy. How dare they then turn round and say that war is wicked?

It is quite true that the English are hypocritical about their Empire. In the working class this hypocrisy takes the form of not knowing that the Empire exists. But their dislike of standing armies is a perfectly sound instinct. A navy employs comparatively few people, and it is an external weapon which cannot affect home politics directly. Military dictatorships exist everywhere, but there is no such thing as a naval dictatorship. What English people of nearly all classes loathe from the bottom of their hearts is the swaggering officer type, the jingle of spurs and the crash of boots. Decades before Hitler was ever heard of, the word 'Prussian' had much the same significance in England as 'Nazi' has today. So deep does this feeling go that for a hundred years past the officers of the British army, in peace time, have always worn civilian clothes when off duty.

One rapid but fairly sure guide to the social atmosphere of a country is the parade-step of its army. A military parade is really a kind of ritual dance, something like a ballet, expressing a certain philosophy of life. The goose-step, for instance, is one of the most horrible sights in the world, far more terrifying than a dive-bomber. It is simply an affirmation of naked power; contained in it, quite consciously and intentionally, is the vision of a boot crashing down on a face. Its ugliness is part of its essence, for what it is saying is 'Yes, I *am* ugly, and you daren't laugh at me', like the bully who makes faces at his victim. Why is the goose-step not used in England? There are, heaven knows, plenty of army officers who would be only too glad to introduce some such thing. It is not used because the people in the street would laugh. Beyond a certain point, military display is only possible in countries where the common people dare not laugh at the army. The Italians adopted the goose-step at about the time when Italy passed definitely under German control, and, as one would expect, they do it less well than the Germans. The Vichy government, if it survives, is bound to introduce a stiffer parade-ground discipline into what is left of the French army. In the British army the drill is rigid and complicated, full of memories of the eighteenth century, but without definite swagger; the march is merely a formalized walk. It belongs to a society which is ruled by the sword, no doubt, but a sword which must never be taken out of the scabbard.

And yet the gentleness of English civilization is mixed up with barbarities and anachronisms. Our criminal law is as out-of-date as the muskets in the Tower. Over against the Nazi Storm Trooper you have got to set that typically English figure, the hanging judge, some gouty old bully with his mind rooted in the nineteenth century, handing out savage sentences. In England people are still hanged by the neck and flogged with the cat o' nine tails. Both of these punishments are obscene as well as cruel, but there has never been any genuinely popular outcry against them. People accept them (and Dartmoor, and Borstal) almost as they accept the weather. They are part of 'the law', which is assumed to be unalterable.

Here one comes upon an all-important English trait: the respect for constitutionalism and legality, the belief in 'the law' as something above the State and above the individual, something which is cruel and stupid, of course, but at any rate *incorruptible*.

It is not that anyone imagines the law to be just. Everyone knows that there is one law for the rich and another for the poor. But no one accepts the implications of this, everyone takes it for granted that the law, such as it is, will be respected, and feels a sense of outrage when it is not. Remarks like 'They can't run me in; I haven't done anything wrong', or 'They can't do that; it's against the law', are part of the atmosphere of England. The professed enemies of society have this feeling as strongly as anyone else. One sees it in prison-books like Wilfred Macartney's *Walls Have Mouths* or Jim Phelan's *Jail Journey*, in the solemn idiocies that take place at the trials of conscientious objectors, in letters to the papers from eminent Marxist professors, pointing out that this or that is a 'miscarriage of British justice'. Everyone believes in his heart that the law can be, ought to be, and, on the whole, will be impartially administered. The totalitarian idea that there is no such thing as law, there is only power, has never taken root. Even the intelligentsia have only accepted it in theory.

An illusion can become a half-truth, a mask can alter the expression of a face. The familiar arguments to the effect that democracy is 'just the same as' or 'just as bad as' totalitarianism never take account of this fact. All such arguments boil down to saying that half a loaf is the same as no bread. In England such concepts as justice, liberty and objective truth are still believed in. They may be illusions, but they are very powerful illusions. The belief in them influences conduct, national life is different because of them. In proof of which, look about you. Where are the rubber truncheons, where is the castor oil? The sword is still in the scabbard, and while it stays there corruption cannot go beyond a certain point. The English electoral system, for instance, is an all but open fraud. In a dozen obvious ways it is gerrymandered in the interest of the moneyed class. But until some deep change has occurred in the public mind, it cannot become *completely* corrupt. You do not arrive at the polling booth to find men with revolvers telling you which way to vote, nor are the votes miscounted, nor is there any direct bribery. Even hypocrisy is a powerful safeguard. The hanging judge, that evil old man in scarlet robe and horse-hair wig, whom nothing short of dynamite will ever teach what century he is living in, but who will at any rate interpret the law according to the books and will in no circumstances take a money bribe, is one of the symbolic figures of England. He is a symbol of the strange mixture of reality and illusion, democracy and privilege, humbug and decency, the subtle network of compromises, by which the nation keeps itself in its familiar shape.

III

I have spoken all the while of 'the nation', 'England', 'Britain', as though forty-five million souls could somehow be treated as a unit. But is not England notoriously two nations, the rich and the poor? Dare one pretend that there is anything in common between people with £100,000 a year and people with £1 a week? And even Welsh and Scottish readers are likely to have been offended because I have used the word 'England' oftener than 'Britain', as though the whole population dwelt in London and the Home Counties and neither north nor west possessed a culture of its own.

One gets a better view of this question if one considers the minor point first. It is quite true that the so-called races of Britain feel themselves to be very different from one another A Scotsman, for instance, does not thank you if you call him an Englishman. You can see the hesitation we feel on this point by the fact that we call our islands by no less than six different names, England, Britain, Great Britain, the British Isles, the United Kingdom and, in very exalted moments, Albion. Even the differences between north and south England loom large in our own eyes. But somehow these differences fade away the moment that any two Britons are confronted by a European. It is very rare to meet a foreigner, other than an American, who can distinguish between English and Scots or even English and Irish. To a Frenchman, the Breton and the Auvergnat seem very different beings, and the accent of Marseilles is a stock joke in Paris. Yet we speak of 'France' and 'the French', recognizing France as an entity, a single civilization, which in fact it is. So also with ourselves. Looked at from the outside, even the cockney and the Yorkshireman have a strong family resemblance.

And even the distinction between rich and poor dwindles somewhat when one regards the nation from the outside. There is no question about the inequality of wealth in England. It is grosser than in any European country, and you have only to look down the nearest street to see it. Economically, England is certainly two nations, if not three or four. But at the same time the vast majority of the people *feel* themselves to be a single nation and are conscious of resembling one another more than they resemble foreigners. Patriotism is usually stronger than class-hatred, and always stronger than any kind of internationalism. Except for a brief moment in 1920 (the 'Hands off Russia' movement) the British working class have never thought or acted internationally. For two and a half years they watched their comrades in Spain slowly strangled, and never aided them by even a single strike.[2] But when their own country (the country of Lord Nuffield and Mr Montagu Norman) was in danger, their attitude was very different. At the moment when it seemed likely that England might be

---

2. It is true that they aided them to a certain extent with money. Still the sums raised for the various aid-Spain funds would not equal five per cent of the turnover of the football pools during the same period. [Author's footnote.]

invaded, Anthony Eden appealed over the radio for Local Defence Volunteers. He got a quarter of a million men in the first twenty-four hours, and another million in the subsequent month. One has only to compare these figures with, for instance, the number of conscientious objectors to see how vast is the strength of traditional loyalties compared with new ones.

In England patriotism takes different forms in different classes, but it runs like a connecting thread through nearly all of them. Only the Europeanized intelligentsia are really immune to it. As a positive emotion it is stronger in the middle class than in the upper class – the cheap public schools, for instance, are more given to patriotic demonstrations than the expensive ones – but the number of definitely treacherous rich men, the Laval–Quisling type is probably very small. In the working class patriotism is profound, but it is unconscious. The working man's heart does not leap when he sees a Union Jack. But the famous 'insularity' and 'xenophobia' of the English is far stronger in the working class than in the bourgeoisie. In all countries the poor are more national than the rich, but the English working class are outstanding in their abhorrence of foreign habits. Even when they are obliged to live abroad for years they refuse either to accustom themselves to foreign food or to learn foreign languages. Nearly every Englishman of working-class origin considers it effeminate to pronounce a foreign word correctly. During the war of 1914–18 the English working class were in contact with foreigners to an extent that is rarely possible. The sole result was that they brought back a hatred of all Europeans, except the Germans, whose courage they admired. In four years on French soil they did not even acquire a liking for wine. The insularity of the English, their refusal to take foreigners seriously, is a folly that has to be paid for very heavily from time to time.

But it plays its part in the English mystique, and the intellectuals who have tried to break it down have generally done more harm than good. At bottom it is the same quality in the English character that repels the tourist and keeps out the invader.

Here one comes back to two English characteristics that I pointed out, seemingly at random, at the beginning of the last chapter. One is the lack of artistic ability. This is perhaps another way of saying that the English are outside the European culture. For there is one art in which they have shown plenty of talent, namely literature. But this is also the only art that cannot cross frontiers. Literature, especially poetry, and lyric poetry most of all, is a kind of family joke, with little or no value outside its own language-group. Except for Shakespeare, the best English poets are barely known in Europe, even as names. The only poets who are widely read are Byron, who is admired for the wrong reasons, and Oscar Wilde, who is pitied as a victim of English hypocrisy. And linked up with this, though not very obviously, is the lack of philosophical faculty, the absence in nearly all Englishmen of any need for an ordered system of thought or even for the use of logic.

Up to a point, the sense of national unity is a substitute for a 'world-view'. Just because patriotism is all but universal and not even the rich are uninfluenced by it, there can be moments when the whole nation suddenly swings together and does the same thing, like a herd of cattle facing a wolf. There was such a moment, unmistakably, at the time of the disaster in France. After eight months of vaguely wondering what the war was about, the people suddenly knew what they had got to do: first to get the army away from Dunkirk, and secondly to prevent invasion. It was like the awakening of a giant. Quick! Danger! The Philistines be upon thee, Samson! And then the swift unanimous action – and then, alas, the prompt relapse into sleep. In a divided nation that would have been exactly the moment for a big peace movement to arise. But does this mean that the instinct of the English will always tell them to do the right thing? Not at all, merely that it will tell them to do the same thing. In the 1931 General Election, for instance, we all did the wrong thing in perfect unison. We were as single-minded as the Gadarene swine. But I honestly doubt whether we can say that we were shoved down the slope against our will.

It follows that British democracy is less of a fraud than it sometimes appears. A foreign observer sees only the huge inequality of wealth, the unfair electoral system, the governing-class control over the press, the radio and education, and concludes that democracy is simply a polite name for dictatorship. But this ignores the considerable agreement that does unfortunately exist between the leaders and the led. However much one may hate to admit it, it is almost certain that between 1931 and 1940 the National Government represented the will of the mass of the people. It tolerated slums, unemployment and a cowardly foreign policy. Yes, but so did public opinion. It was a stagnant period, and its natural leaders were mediocrities.

In spite of the campaigns of a few thousand left-wingers, it is fairly certain that the bulk of the English people were behind Chamberlain's foreign policy. More, it is fairly certain that the same struggle was going on in Chamberlain's mind as in the minds of ordinary people. His opponents professed to see in him a dark and wily schemer, plotting to sell England to Hitler, but it is far likelier that he was merely a stupid old man doing his best according to his very dim lights. It is difficult otherwise to explain the contradictions of his policy, his failure to grasp any of the courses that were open to him. Like the mass of the people, he did not want to pay the price either of peace or of war. And public opinion was behind him all the while, in policies that were completely incompatible with one another. It was behind him when he went to Munich, when he tried to come to an understanding with Russia, when he gave the guarantee to Poland, when he honoured it, and when he prosecuted the war half-heartedly. Only when the results of his policy became apparent did it turn against him; which is to say that it turned against its own lethargy of the past seven years. Thereupon the people picked a leader nearer to their mood, Churchill, who was at any rate able to grasp that wars are not won without fighting. Later, perhaps, they will pick another leader who can grasp that only Socialist nations can fight effectively.

Do I mean by all this that England is a genuine democracy? No, not even a reader of the *Daily Telegraph* could quite swallow that.

England is the most class-ridden country under the sun. It is a land of snobbery and privilege, ruled largely by the old and silly. But in any calculation about it one has got to take into account its emotional unity, the tendency of nearly all its inhabitants to feel alike and act together in moments of supreme crisis. It is the only great country in Europe that is not obliged to drive hundreds of thousands of its nationals into exile or the concentration camp. At this moment, after a year of war, newspapers and pamphlets abusing the Government, praising the enemy and clamouring for surrender are being sold on the streets, almost without interference. And this is less from a respect for freedom of speech than from a simple perception that these things don't matter. It is safe to let a paper like *Peace News* be sold, because it is certain that ninety-five per cent of the population will never want to read it. The nation is bound together by an invisible chain. At any normal time the ruling class will rob, mismanage, sabotage, lead us into the muck; but let popular opinion really make itself heard, let them get a tug from below that they cannot avoid feeling, and it is difficult for them not to respond. The left-wing writers who denounce the whole of the ruling class as 'pro-Fascist' are grossly over-simplifying. Even among the inner clique of politicians who brought us to our present pass, it is doubtful whether there were any *conscious* traitors. The corruption that happens in England is seldom of that kind. Nearly always it is more in the nature of self-deception, of the right hand not knowing what the left hand doeth. And being unconscious, it is limited. One sees this at its most obvious in the English press. Is the English press honest or dishonest? At normal times it is deeply dishonest. All the papers that matter live off their advertisements, and the advertisers exercise an indirect censorship over news. Yet I do not suppose there is one paper in England that can be straightforwardly bribed with hard cash. In the France of the Third Republic all but a very few of the newspapers could notoriously be bought over the counter like so many pounds of cheese. Public life in England has never been *openly* scandalous. It has not reached the pitch of disintegration at which humbug can be dropped.

England is not the jewelled isle of Shakespeare's much-quoted message, nor is it the inferno depicted by Dr Goebbels. More than either it resembles a family, a rather stuffy Victorian family, with not many black sheep in it but with all its cupboards bursting with skeletons. It has rich relations who have to be kow-towed to and poor relations who are horribly sat upon, and there is a deep conspiracy of silence about the source of the family income. It is a family in which the young are generally thwarted and most of the power is in the hands of irresponsible uncles and bedridden aunts. Still, it is a family. It has its private language and its common memories, and at the approach of an enemy it closes its ranks. A family with the wrong members in control – that, perhaps, is as near as one can come to describing England in a phrase.

IV

Probably the battle of Waterloo *was* won on the playing-fields of Eton, but the opening battles of all subsequent wars have been lost there. One of the dominant facts in English life during the past three quarters of a century has been the decay of ability in the ruling class.

In the years between 1920 and 1940 it was happening with the speed of a chemical reaction. Yet at the moment of writing it is still possible to speak of a ruling class. Like the knife which has two new blades and three new handles, the upper fringe of English society is still almost what it was in the mid nineteenth century. After 1832 the old land-owning aristocracy steadily lost power, but instead of disappearing or becoming a fossil they simply intermarried with the merchants, manufacturers and financiers who had replaced them, and soon turned them into accurate copies of themselves. The wealthy shipowner or cotton-miller set up for himself an alibi as a country gentleman, while his sons learned the right mannerisms at public schools which had been designed for just that purpose. England was ruled by an aristocracy constantly recruited from parvenus. And considering what energy the self-made men possessed, and considering that they were buying their way into a class which at any rate had a tradition of public service, one might have expected that able rulers could be produced in some such way.

And yet somehow the ruling class decayed, lost its ability, its daring, finally even its ruthlessness, until a time came when stuffed shirts like Eden or Halifax could stand out as men of exceptional talent. As for Baldwin, one could not even dignify him with the name of stuffed shirt. He was simply a hole in the air. The mishandling of England's domestic problems during the nineteen-twenties had been bad enough, but British foreign policy between 1931 and 1939 is one of the wonders of the world. Why? What had happened? What was it that at every decisive moment made every British statesman do the wrong thing with so unerring an instinct?

The underlying fact was that the whole position of the moneyed class had long ceased to be justifiable. There they sat, at the centre of a vast empire and a world-wide financial network, drawing interest and profits and spending them – on what? It was fair to say that life within the British Empire was in many ways better than life outside it. Still, the Empire was under-developed, India slept in the Middle Ages, the Dominions lay empty, with foreigners jealously barred out, and even England was full of slums and unemployment. Only half a million people, the people in the country houses, definitely benefited from the existing system. Moreover, the tendency of small businesses to merge together into large ones robbed more and more of the moneyed class of their function and turned them into mere *owners*, their work being done for them by salaried managers and technicians. For long past there had been in England an entirely functionless class, living on money that was invested they hardly knew where, the 'idle rich', the people whose photographs you can look at in the *Tatler* and the *Bystander*, always supposing that you want to. The existence of these people was by any standard unjustifiable. They were simply parasites, less useful to society than his fleas are to a dog.

By 1920 there were many people who were aware of all this. By 1930 millions were aware of it. But the British ruling class obviously could not admit to themselves that their usefulness was at an end. Had they done that they would have had to abdicate. For it was not possible for them to turn themselves into mere bandits, like the American millionaires, consciously clinging to unjust privileges and beating down opposition by bribery and tear-gas bombs. After all, they belonged to a class with a certain tradition, they had been to public schools where the duty of dying for your country, if necessary, is laid down as the first and greatest of the Commandments. They had to *feel* themselves true patriots, even while they plundered their countrymen. Clearly there was only one escape for them – into stupidity. They could keep society in its existing shape only by being *unable* to grasp that any improvement was possible. Difficult though this was, they achieved it, largely by fixing their eyes on the past and refusing to notice the changes that were going on round them.

There is much in England that this explains. It explains the decay of country life, due to the keeping-up of a sham feudalism which drives the more spirited workers off the land. It explains the immobility of the public schools, which have barely altered since the eighties of the last century. It explains the military incompetence which has again and again startled the world. Since the fifties every war in which England has engaged has started off with a series of disasters, after which the situation has been saved by people comparatively low in the social scale. The higher commanders, drawn from the aristocracy, could never prepare for modern war, because in order to do so they would have had to admit to themselves that the world was changing. They have always clung to obsolete methods and weapons, because they inevitably saw each war as a repetition of the last. Before the Boer War they prepared for the Zulu War, before the 1914 for the Boer War, and before the present war for 1914. Even at this moment hundreds of thousands of men in England are being trained with the bayonet, a weapon entirely useless except for opening tins. It is worth noticing that the navy and, latterly, the air force, have always been more efficient than the regular army. But the navy is only partially, and the air, force hardly at all, within the ruling-class orbit

It must be admitted that so long as things were peaceful the methods of the British ruling class served them well enough. Their own people manifestly tolerated them. However unjustly England might be organized, it was at any rate not torn by class warfare or haunted by secret police. The Empire was peaceful as no area of comparable size has ever been. Throughout its vast extent, nearly a quarter of the earth, there were fewer armed men than would be found necessary by a minor Balkan state. As people to live under, and looking at them merely from a liberal, *negative* standpoint, the British ruling class had their points. They were preferable to the truly modern men, the Nazis and Fascists. But it had long been obvious that they would be helpless against any serious attack from the outside.

They could not struggle against Nazism or Fascism, because they could not understand them. Neither could they have struggled against Communism, if Communism had been a serious force in western Europe. To understand Fascism they would have had to study the theory of Socialism, which would have forced them to realize that the economic system by which they lived was unjust, inefficient and out-of-date. But it was exactly this fact that they had trained themselves never to face. They dealt with Fascism as the cavalry generals of 1914 dealt with the machine-guns – by ignoring it. After years of aggression and massacres, they had grasped only one fact, that Hitler and Mussolini were hostile to Communism. Therefore, it was argued, they *must* be friendly to the British dividend-drawer. Hence the truly frightening spectacle of Conservative M.P.s wildly cheering the news that British ships, bringing food to the Spanish Republican government, had been bombed by Italian aeroplanes. Even when they had begun to grasp that Fascism was dangerous, its essentially revolutionary nature, the huge military effort it was capable of making, the sort of tactics it would use, were quite beyond their comprehension. At the time of the Spanish Civil War, anyone with as much political knowledge as can be acquired from a sixpenny pamphlet on Socialism knew that, if Franco won, the result would be strategically disastrous for England; and yet generals and admirals who had given their lives to the study of war were unable to grasp this fact. This vein of political ignorance runs right through English official life, through Cabinet ministers, ambassadors, consuls, judges, magistrates, policemen. The policeman who arrests the 'red' does not understand the theories the 'red' is preaching; if he did his own position as bodyguard of the moneyed class might seem less pleasant to him. There is reason to think that even military espionage is hopelessly hampered by ignorance of the new economic doctrines and the ramifications of the underground parties.

The British ruling class were not altogether wrong in thinking that Fascism was on their side. It is a fact that any rich man, unless he is a Jew, has less to fear from Fascism than from either Communism or democratic Socialism. One ought never to forget this, for nearly the whole of German and Italian propaganda is designed to cover it up. The natural instinct of men like Simon, Hoare, Chamberlain etc. was to come to an agreement with Hitler. But – and here the peculiar feature of English life that I have spoken of, the deep sense of national solidarity, comes in – they could only do so by breaking up the Empire and selling their own people into semi-slavery. A truly corrupt class would have done this without hesitation, as in France. But things had not gone that distance in England. Politicians who would make cringing speeches about 'the duty of loyalty to our conquerors' are hardly to be found in English public life. Tossed to and fro between their incomes and their principles, it was impossible that men like Chamberlain should do anything but make the worst of both worlds.

One thing that has always shown that the English ruling class are *morally* fairly sound, is that in time of war they are ready enough to get themselves killed. Several dukes, earls and what nots were killed in the recent campaign in Flanders. That could not happen if these people were the cynical scoundrels that they are sometimes declared to be. It is important not to misunderstand their motives, or one cannot predict their actions. What is to be expected of them is not treachery, or physical cowardice, but stupidity, unconscious sabotage, an infallible instinct for doing the wrong thing. They are not wicked, or not altogether wicked; they are merely unteachable. Only when their money and power are gone will the younger among them begin to grasp what century they are living in.

V

The stagnation of the Empire in the between-war years affected everyone in England, but it had an especially direct effect upon two important sub-sections of the middle class. One was the military and imperialist middle class, generally nicknamed the Blimps, and the other the left-wing intelligentsia. These two seemingly hostile types, symbolic opposites – the half-pay colonel with his bull neck and diminutive brain, like a dinosaur, the highbrow with his domed forehead and stalk-like neck – are mentally linked together and constantly interact upon one another; in any case they are born to a considerable extent into the same families.

Thirty years ago the Blimp class was already losing its vitality. The middle-class families celebrated by Kipling, the prolific lowbrow families whose sons officered the army and navy and swarmed over all the waste places of the earth from the Yukon to the Irrawaddy, were dwindling before 1914. The thing that had killed them was the telegraph. In a narrowing world, more and more governed from Whitehall, there was every year less room for individual initiative. Men like Clive, Nelson, Nicholson, Gordon would find no place for themselves in the modern British Empire. By 1920 nearly every inch of the colonial empire was in the grip of Whitehall. Well-meaning, over-civilized men, in dark suits and black felt hats, with neatly rolled umbrellas crooked over the left forearm, were imposing their constipated view of life on Malaya and Nigeria, Mombasa and Mandalay. The one-time empire builders were reduced to the status of clerks, buried deeper and deeper under mounds of paper and red tape. In the early twenties one could see, all over the Empire, the older officials, who had known more spacious days, writhing impotently under the changes that were happening. From that time onwards it has been next door to impossible to induce young men of spirit to take any part in imperial administration. And what was true of the official world was true also of the commercial. The great monopoly companies swallowed up hosts of petty traders. Instead of going out to trade adventurously in the Indies one went to an office stool in Bombay or Singapore. And life in Bombay or Singapore was actually duller and safer than life in London. Imperialist sentiment remained strong in the middle class, chiefly owing to family tradition, but the job of administering the Empire had ceased to appeal. Few able men went east of Suez if there was any way of avoiding it.

But the general weakening of imperialism, and to some extent of the whole British morale, that took place during the nineteen-thirties, was partly the work of the left-wing intelligentsia, itself a kind of growth that had sprouted from the stagnation of the Empire.

It should be noted that there is now no intelligentsia that is not in some sense 'left'. Perhaps the last right-wing intellectual was T. E. Lawrence. Since about 1930 everyone describable as an 'intellectual' has lived in a state of chronic discontent with the existing order. Necessarily so, because society as it was constituted had no room for him. In an Empire that was simply stagnant, neither being developed nor falling to pieces, and in an England ruled by people whose chief asset was their stupidity, to be 'clever' was to be suspect. If you had the kind of brain that could understand the poems of T. S. Eliot or the theories of Karl Marx, the higher-ups would see to it that you were kept out of any important job. The intellectuals could find a function for themselves only in the literary reviews and the left-wing political parties.

The mentality of the English left-wing intelligentsia can be studied in half a dozen weekly and monthly papers. The immediately striking thing about all these papers is their generally negative, querulous attitude, their complete lack at all times of any constructive suggestion. There is little in them except the irresponsible carping of people who have never been and never expect to be in a position of power. Another marked characteristic is the emotional shallowness of people who live in a world of ideas and have little contact with physical reality. Many intellectuals of the Left were flabbily pacifist up to 1935, shrieked for war against Germany in the years 1935-9, and then promptly cooled off when the war started. It is broadly though not precisely true that the people who were most 'anti-Fascist' during the Spanish Civil War are most defeatist now. And underlying this is the really important fact about so many of the English intelligentsia – their severance from the common culture of the country.

In intention, at any rate, the English intelligentsia are Europeanized. They take their cookery from Paris and their opinions from Moscow. In the general patriotism of the country they form a sort of island of dissident thought. England is perhaps the only great country whose intellectuals are ashamed of their own nationality. In left-wing circles it is always felt that there is something slightly disgraceful in being an Englishman and that it is a duty to snigger at every English institution, from horse racing to suet puddings. It is a strange fact, but it is unquestionably true that almost any English intellectual would feel more ashamed of standing to attention during 'God save the King' than of stealing from a poor box. All through the critical years many left-wingers were chipping away at English morale, trying to spread an outlook that was sometimes squashily pacifist, sometimes violently pro-Russian, but always anti-British. It is questionable how much effect this had, but it certainly had some. If the English people suffered for several years a real weakening of morale, so that the Fascist nations judged that they were 'decadent' and that it was safe to plunge into war, the intellectual sabotage from the Left was partly responsible. Both the *New Statesman* and the *News Chronicle* cried out against the Munich settlement, but even they had done something to make it possible. Ten years of systematic Blimp-baiting affected even the Blimps themselves and made it harder than it had been before to get intelligent young men to enter the armed forces. Given the stagnation of the Empire the military middle class must have decayed in any case, but the spread of a shallow Leftism hastened the process.

It is clear that the special position of the English intellectuals during the past ten years, as purely *negative* creatures, mere anti-Blimps, was a by-product of ruling-class stupidity. Society could not use them, and they had not got it in them to see that devotion to one's country implies 'for better, for worse'. Both Blimps and highbrows took for granted, as though it were a law of nature, the divorce between patriotism and intelligence. If you were a patriot you read *Blackwood's Magazine* and publicly thanked God that you were 'not brainy'. If you were an intellectual you sniggered at the Union Jack and regarded physical courage as barbarous. It is obvious that this preposterous convention cannot continue. The Bloomsbury highbrow, with his mechanical snigger, is as out-of-date as the cavalry colonel. A modern nation cannot afford either of them. Patriotism and intelligence will have to come together again. It is the fact that we are fighting a war, and a very peculiar kind of war, that may make this possible.

VI

One of the most important developments in England during the past twenty years has been the upward and downward extension of the middle class. It has happened on such a scale as to make the old classification of society into capitalists, proletarians and petit bourgeois (small property-owners) almost obsolete.

England is a country in which property and financial power are concentrated in very few hands. Few people in modern England *own* anything at all, except clothes, furniture and possibly a house. The peasantry have long since disappeared, the independent shopkeeper is being destroyed, the small businessman is diminishing in numbers. But at the same time modern industry is so complicated that it cannot get along without great numbers of managers, salesmen, engineers, chemists and technicians of all kinds, drawing fairly large salaries. And these in turn call into being a professional class of doctors, lawyers, teachers, artists, etc. etc. The tendency of advanced capitalism has therefore been to enlarge the middle class and not to wipe it out as it once seemed likely to do.

But much more important than this is the spread of middle-class ideas and habits among the working class. The British working class are now better off in almost all ways than they were thirty years ago. This is partly due to the efforts of the trade unions, but partly to the mere advance of physical science. It is not always realized that within rather narrow limits the standard of life of a country can rise without a corresponding rise in real wages. Up to a point, civilization can lift itself up by its boot-tags. However unjustly society is organized, certain technical advances are bound to benefit the whole community, because certain kinds of goods are necessarily held in common. A millionaire cannot, for example, light the streets for himself while darkening them for other people. Nearly all citizens of civilized countries now enjoy the use of good roads, germ-free water, police protection, free libraries and probably free education of a kind. Public education in England has been meanly starved of money, but it has nevertheless improved, largely owing to the devoted efforts of the teachers, and the habit of reading has become enormously more widespread. To an increasing extent the rich and the poor read the same books, and they also see the same films and listen to the same radio programmes. And the differences in their way of life have been diminished by the mass-production of cheap clothes and improvements in housing. So far as outward appearance goes, the clothes of rich and poor, especially in the case of women, differ far less than they did thirty or even fifteen years ago. As to housing, England still has slums which are a blot on civilization, but much building has been done during the past ten years, largely by the local authorities. The modern council house, with its bathroom and electric light, is smaller than the stockbroker's villa, but it is recognizably the same kind of house, which the farm labourer's cottage is not. A person who has grown up in a council housing estate is likely to be – indeed, visibly *is* – more middle class in outlook than a person who has grown up in a slum.

The effect of all this is a general softening of manners. It is enhanced by the fact that modern industrial methods tend always to demand less muscular effort and therefore to leave people with more energy when their day's work is done. Many workers in the light industries are less truly manual labourers than is a doctor or a grocer. In tastes, habits, manners and outlook the working class and the middle class are drawing together. The unjust distinctions remain, but the real differences diminish. The old-style 'proletarian' – collarless, unshaven and with muscles warped by heavy labour – still exists, but he is constantly decreasing in numbers; he only predominates in the heavy-industry areas of the north of England.

After 1918 there began to appear something that had never existed in England before: people of indeterminate social class. In 1910 every human being in these islands could be 'placed' in an instant by his clothes, manners and accent. That is no longer the case. Above all, it is not the case in the new townships that have developed as a result of cheap motor cars and the southward shift of industry. The place to look for the germs of the future England is in light-industry areas and along the arterial roads. In Slough, Dagenham, Barnet, Letchworth, Hayes – everywhere, indeed, on the outskirts of great towns – the old pattern is gradually changing into something new. In those vast new wildernesses of glass and brick the sharp distinctions of the older kind of town, with its slums and mansions, or of the country, with its manor-houses and squalid cottages, no longer exist. There are wide gradations of income, but it is the same kind of life that is being lived at different levels, in labour-saving flats or council houses, along the concrete roads and in the naked democracy of the swimming-pools. It is a rather restless, cultureless life, centring round tinned food, *Picture Post*, the radio and the internal combustion engine. It is a civilization in which children grow up with an intimate knowledge of magnetoes and in complete ignorance of the Bible. To that civilization belong the people who are most at home in and most definitely *of* the modern world, the technicians and the higher-paid skilled workers, the airmen and their mechanics, the radio experts, film producers, popular journalists and industrial chemists. They are the indeterminate stratum at which the older class distinctions are beginning to break down.

This war, unless we are defeated, will wipe out most of the existing class privileges. There are every day fewer people who wish them to continue. Nor need we fear that as the pattern changes life in England will lose its peculiar flavour. The new red cities of Greater London are crude enough, but these things are only the rash that accompanies a change. In whatever shape England emerges from the war it will be deeply tinged with the characteristics that I have spoken of earlier. The intellectuals who hope to see it Russianized or Germanized will be disappointed. The gentleness, the hypocrisy, the thoughtlessness, the reverence for law and the hatred of uniforms will remain, along with the suet puddings and the misty skies. It needs some very great disaster, such as prolonged subjugation by a foreign enemy, to destroy a national culture. The Stock Exchange will be pulled down, the horse plough will give way to the tractor, the country houses will be turned into children's holiday camps, the Eton and Harrow match will be forgotten, but England will still be England, an everlasting animal stretching into the future and the past, and, like all living things, having the power to change out of recognition and yet remain the same.

PART TWO:

Shopkeepers at War

I

I began this book to the tune of German bombs, and I begin this second chapter in the added racket of the barrage. The yellow gun-flashes are lighting the sky, the splinters are rattling on the housetops, and London Bridge is falling down, falling down, falling down. Anyone able to read a map knows that we are in deadly danger. I do not mean that we are beaten or need be beaten. Almost certainly the outcome depends on our own will. But at this moment we are in the soup, full fathom five, and we have been brought there by follies which we are still committing and which will drown us altogether if we do not mend our ways quickly.

What this war has demonstrated is that private capitalism – that is, an economic system in which land, factories, mines and transport are owned privately and operated solely for profit – *does not work*. It cannot deliver the goods. This fact had been known to millions of people for years past, but nothing ever came of it, because there was no real urge from below to alter the system, and those at the top had trained themselves to be impenetrably stupid on just this point. Argument and propaganda got one nowhere. The lords of property simply sat on their bottoms and proclaimed that all was for the best. Hitler's conquest of Europe, however, was a *physical* debunking of capitalism. War, for all its evil, is at any rate an unanswerable test of strength, like a try-your-grip machine. Great strength returns the penny, and there is no way of faking the result.

When the nautical screw was first invented, there was a controversy that lasted for years as to whether screw-steamers or paddle-steamers were better. The paddle-steamers, like all obsolete things, had their champions, who supported them by ingenious arguments. Finally, however, a distinguished admiral tied a screw-steamer and a paddle-steamer of equal horsepower stern to stern and set their engines running. That settled the question once and for all. And it was something similar that happened on the fields of Norway and of Flanders. Once and for all it was proved that a planned economy is stronger than a planless one. But it is necessary here to give some kind of definition to those much-abused words, Socialism and Fascism.

Socialism is usually defined as 'common ownership of the means of production'. Crudely: the State, representing the whole nation, owns everything, and everyone is a State employee. This does *not* mean that people are stripped of private possessions such as clothes and furniture, but it *does* mean that all productive goods, such as land, mines, ships and machinery, are the property of the State. The State is the sole large-scale producer. It is not certain that Socialism is in all ways superior to capitalism, but it is certain that, unlike capitalism, it can solve the problems of production and consumption. At normal times a capitalist economy can never consume all that it produces, so that there is always a wasted surplus (wheat burned in furnaces, herrings dumped back into the sea etc. etc.) and always unemployment. In time of war, on the other hand, it has difficulty in producing all that it needs, because nothing is produced unless someone sees his way to making a profit out of it.

In a Socialist economy these problems do not exist. The State simply calculates what goods will be needed and does its best to produce them. Production is only limited by the amount of labour and raw materials. Money, for internal purposes, ceases to be a mysterious all-powerful thing and becomes a sort of coupon or ration-ticket, issued in sufficient quantities to buy up such consumption goods as may be available at the moment.

However, it has become clear in the last few years that 'common ownership of the means of production' is not in itself a sufficient definition of Socialism. One must also add the following: approximate equality of incomes (it need be no more than approximate), political democracy, and abolition of all hereditary privilege, especially in education. These are simply the necessary safeguards against the reappearance of a class-system. Centralized ownership has very little meaning unless the mass of the people are living roughly upon an equal level, and have some kind of control over the government. 'The State' may come to mean no more than a self-elected political party, and oligarchy and privilege can return, based on power rather than on money.

But what then is Fascism?

Fascism, at any rate the German version, is a form of capitalism that borrows from Socialism just such features as will make it efficient for war purposes. Internally, Germany has a good deal in common with a Socialist state. Ownership has never been abolished, there are still capitalists and workers, and – this is the important point, and the real reason why rich men all over the world tend to sympathize with Fascism – generally speaking the same people are capitalists and the same people workers as before the Nazi revolution. But at the same time the State, which is simply the Nazi Party, is in control of everything. It controls investment, raw materials, rates of interest, working hours, wages. The factory owner still owns his factory, but he is for practical purposes reduced to the status of a manager. Everyone is in effect a State employee, though the salaries vary very greatly. The mere *efficiency* of such a system, the elimination of waste and obstruction, is obvious. In seven years it has built up the most powerful war machine the world has ever seen.

But the idea underlying Fascism is irreconcilably different from that which underlies Socialism. Socialism aims, ultimately, at a world-state of free and equal human beings. It takes the equality of human rights for granted. Nazism assumes just the opposite. The driving force behind the Nazi movement is the belief in human *inequality*, the superiority of Germans to all other races, the right of Germany to rule the world. Outside the German Reich it does not recognize any obligations. Eminent Nazi professors have 'proved' over and over again that only nordic man is fully human, have even mooted the idea that non-nordic peoples (such as ourselves) can interbreed with gorillas! Therefore, while a species of war-Socialism exists within the German state, its attitude towards conquered nations is frankly that of an exploiter. The function of the Czechs, Poles, French, etc. is simply to produce such goods as Germany may need, and get in return just as little as will keep them from open rebellion. If we are conquered, our job will probably be to manufacture weapons for Hitler's forthcoming wars with Russia and America. The

Nazis aim, in effect, at setting up a kind of caste system, with four main castes corresponding rather closely to those of the Hindu religion. At the top comes the Nazi party, second come the mass of the German people, third come the conquered European populations. Fourth and last are to come the coloured peoples, the 'semi-apes' as Hitler calls them, who are to be reduced quite openly to slavery.

However horrible this system may seem to us, *it works*. It works because it is a planned system geared to a definite purpose, world-conquest, and not allowing any private interest, either of capitalist or worker, to stand in its way. British capitalism does not work, because it is a competitive system in which private profit is and must be the main objective. It is a system in which all the forces are pulling in opposite directions and the interests of the individual are as often as not totally opposed to those of the State.

All through the critical years British capitalism, with its immense industrial plant and its unrivalled supply of skilled labour, was unequal to the strain of preparing for war. To prepare for war on the modern scale you have got to divert the greater part of your national income to armaments, which means cutting down on consumption goods. A bombing plane, for instance, is equivalent in price to fifty small motor cars, or eight thousand pairs of silk stockings, or a million loaves of bread. Clearly you can't have *many* bombing planes without lowering the national standard of life. It is guns or butter, as Marshal Goering remarked. But in Chamberlain's England the transition could not be made. The rich would not face the necessary taxation, and while the rich are still visibly rich it is not possible to tax the poor very heavily either. Moreover, so long as *profit* was the main object the manufacturer had no incentive to change over from consumption goods to armaments. A businessman's first duty is to his shareholders. Perhaps England needs tanks, but perhaps it pays better to manufacture motor cars. To prevent war material from reaching the enemy is common sense, but to sell in the highest market is a business duty. Right at the end of August 1939 the British dealers were tumbling over one another in their eagerness to sell Germany tin, rubber, copper and shellac – and this in the clear, certain knowledge that war was going to break out in a week or two. It was about as sensible as selling somebody a razor to cut your throat with. But it was 'good business'.

And now look at the results. After 1934 it was known that Germany was rearming. After 1936 everyone with eyes in his head knew that war was coming. After Munich it was merely a question of how soon the war would begin. In September 1939 war broke out. *Eight months later* it was discovered that, so far as equipment went, the British army was barely beyond the standard of 1918. We saw our soldiers fighting their way desperately to the coast, with one aeroplane against three, with rifles against tanks, with bayonets against tommy-guns. There were not even enough revolvers to supply all the officers. After a year of war the regular army was still short of 300,000 tin hats. There had even, previously, been a shortage of uniforms – this in one of the greatest woollen-goods producing countries in the world!

What had happened was that the whole moneyed class, unwilling to face a change in their way of life, had shut their eyes to the nature of Fascism and modern war. And false optimism was fed to the general public by the gutter press, which lives on its advertisements and is therefore interested in keeping trade conditions normal. Year after year the Beaverbrook press assured us in huge headlines that THERE WILL BE NO WAR, and as late as the beginning of 1939 Lord

Rothermere was describing Hitler as 'a great gentleman'. And while England in the moment of disaster proved to be short of every war material except ships, it is not recorded that there was any shortage of motor cars, fur coats, gramophones, lipstick, chocolates or silk stockings. And dare anyone pretend that the same tug-of-war between private profit and public necessity is not still continuing? England fights for her life, but business must fight for profits. You can hardly open a newspaper without seeing the two contradictory processes happening side by side. On the very same page you will find the Government urging you to save and the seller of some useless luxury urging you to spend. Lend to Defence, but Guinness is Good for You. Buy a Spitfire, but also buy Haig and Haig, Pond's Face Cream and Black Magic Chocolates.

But one thing gives hope — the visible swing in public opinion. If we can survive this war, the defeat in Flanders will turn out to have been one of the great turning-points in English history. In that spectacular disaster the working class, the middle class and even a section of the business community could see the utter rottenness of private capitalism. Before that the case against capitalism had never been *proved*. Russia, the only definitely Socialist country, was backward and far away. All criticism broke itself against the rat-trap faces of bankers and the brassy laughter of stockbrokers. Socialism? Ha! ha! ha! Where's the money to come from? Ha! ha! ha! The lords of property were firm in their seats, and they knew it. But after the French collapse there came something that could not be laughed away, something that neither cheque-books nor policemen were any use against — the bombing. Zweee – BOOM! What's that? Oh, only a bomb on the Stock Exchange. Zweee – BOOM! Another acre of somebody's valuable slum-property gone west. Hitler will at any rate go down in history as the man who made the City of London laugh on the wrong side of its face. For the first time in their lives the comfortable were uncomfortable, the professional optimists had to admit that there was something wrong. It was a great step forward. From that time onwards the ghastly job of trying to convince artificially stupefied people that a planned economy might be better than a free-for-all in which the worst man wins – that job will never be quite so ghastly again.

II

The difference between Socialism and capitalism is not primarily a difference of technique. One cannot simply change from one system to the other as one might install a new piece of machinery in a factory, and then carry on as before, with the same people in positions of control. Obviously there is also needed a complete shift of power. New blood, new men, new ideas – in the true sense of the word, a revolution.

I have spoken earlier of the soundness and homogeneity of England, the patriotism that runs like a connecting thread through almost all classes. After Dunkirk anyone who had eyes in his head could see this. But it is absurd to pretend that the promise of that moment has been fulfilled. Almost certainly the mass of the people are now ready for the vast changes that are necessary; but those changes have not even begun to happen.

England is a family with the wrong members in control. Almost entirely we are governed by the rich, and by people who step into positions of command by right of birth. Few if any of these people are consciously treacherous, some of them are not even fools, but as a class they are quite incapable of leading us to victory. They could not do it, even if their material interests did not constantly trip them up. As I pointed out earlier, they have been artificially stupefied. Quite apart from anything else, the rule of money sees to it that we shall be governed largely by the old – that is, by people utterly unable to grasp what age they are living in or what enemy they are fighting. Nothing was more desolating at the beginning of this war than the way in which the whole of the older generation conspired to pretend that it was the war of 1914–18 over again. All the old duds were back on the job, twenty years older, with the skull plainer in their faces. Ian Hay was cheering up the troops, Belloc was writing articles on strategy, Maurois doing broadcasts, Bairnsfather drawing cartoons. It was like a tea-party of ghosts. And that state of affairs has barely altered. The shock of disaster brought a few able men like Bevin to the front, but in general we are still commanded by people who managed to live through the years 1931–9 without even discovering that Hitler was dangerous. A generation of the unteachable is hanging upon us like a necklace of corpses.

As soon as one considers any problem of this war – and it does not matter whether it is the widest aspect of strategy or the tiniest detail of home organization – one sees that the necessary moves cannot be made while the social structure of England remains what it is. Inevitably, because of their position and upbringing, the ruling class are fighting for their own privileges, which cannot possibly be reconciled with the public interest. It is a mistake to imagine that war aims, strategy, propaganda and industrial organization exist in watertight compartments. All are interconnected. Every strategic plan, every tactical method, even every weapon will bear the stamp of the social system that produced it. The British ruling class are fighting against Hitler, whom they have always regarded and whom some of them still regard as their protector against Bolshevism. That does not mean that they will deliberately sell out; but it does mean that at every decisive moment they are likely to falter, pull their punches, do the wrong thing.

Until the Churchill Government called some sort of halt to the process, they have done the wrong thing with an unerring instinct ever since 1931. They helped Franco to overthrow the Spanish Government, although anyone not an imbecile could have told them that a Fascist Spain would be hostile to England. They fed Italy with war materials all through the winter of 1939–40, although it was obvious to the whole world that the Italians were going to attack us in the spring. For the sake of a few hundred thousand dividend-drawers they are turning India from an ally into an enemy. Moreover, so long as the moneyed classes remain in control, we cannot develop any but a *defensive* strategy. Every victory means a change in the *status quo*. How can we drive the Italians out of Abyssinia without rousing echoes among the coloured peoples of our own Empire? How can we even smash Hitler without the risk of bringing the German Socialists and Communists into power? The left-wingers who wail that 'this is a capitalist war' and that 'British Imperialism' is fighting for loot have got their heads screwed on backwards. The last thing the British moneyed class wish for is to acquire fresh territory. It would simply be an embarrassment. Their war aim (both unattainable and unmentionable) is simply to hang on to what they have got.

Internally, England is still the rich man's Paradise. All talk of 'equality of sacrifice' is nonsense. At the same time as factory-workers are asked to put up with longer hours, advertisements for 'Butler. One in family, eight in staff' are appearing in the press. The bombed-out populations of the East End go hungry and homeless while wealthier victims simply step into their cars and flee to comfortable country houses. The Home Guard swells to a million men in a few weeks, and is deliberately organized from above in such a way that only people with private incomes can hold positions of command. Even the rationing system is so arranged that it hits the poor all the time, while people with over £2,000 a year are practically unaffected by it. Everywhere privilege is squandering good will. In such circumstances even propaganda becomes almost impossible. As attempts to stir up patriotic feeling, the red posters issued by the Chamberlain Government at the beginning of the war broke all depth-records. Yet they could not have been much other than they were, for how could Chamberlain and his followers take the risk of rousing strong popular feeling *against Fascism*? Anyone who was genuinely hostile to Fascism must also be opposed to Chamberlain himself and to all the others who had helped Hitler into power. So also with external propaganda. In all Lord Halifax's speeches there is not one concrete proposal for which a single inhabitant of Europe would risk the top joint of his little finger. For what war aim can Halifax, or anyone like him, conceivably have, except to put the clock back to 1933?

It is only by revolution that the native genius of the English people can be set free. Revolution does not mean red flags and street fighting, it means a fundamental shift of power. Whether it happens with or without bloodshed is largely an accident of time and place. Nor does it mean the dictatorship of a single class. The people in England who grasp what changes are needed and are capable of carrying them through are not confined to any one class, though it is true that very few people with over £2,000 a year are among them. What is wanted is a conscious open revolt by ordinary people against inefficiency, class privilege and the rule of the old. It is not primarily a question of change of government. British governments do, broadly speaking, represent the will of the people, and if we alter our structure from below we shall get the government we need. Ambassadors, generals, officials and colonial administrators who are senile or pro-Fascist are more dangerous than Cabinet ministers whose follies have to be committed in public. Right through our national life we have got to fight against privilege, against the notion that a half-witted public-schoolboy is better for command than an intelligent mechanic. Although there are gifted and honest *individuals* among them, we have got to break the grip of the moneyed class as a whole. England has got to assume its real shape. The England that is only just beneath the surface, in the factories and the newspaper offices, in the aeroplanes and the submarines, has got to take charge of its own destiny.

In the short run, equality of sacrifice, 'war-Communism', is even more important than radical economic changes. It is very necessary that industry should be nationalized, but it is more urgently necessary that such monstrosities as butlers and 'private incomes' should disappear forthwith. Almost certainly the main reason why the Spanish Republic could keep up the fight for two and a half years against impossible odds was that there were no gross contrasts of wealth. The people suffered horribly, but they all suffered alike. When the private soldier had not a cigarette, the general had not one either. Given equality of sacrifice, the morale of a country like England would probably be unbreakable. But at present we have nothing to appeal to except traditional patriotism, which is deeper here than elsewhere, but is not necessarily bottomless. At some point or another you have got to deal with the man who says 'I should be no worse off under Hitler.' But what answer can you give him – that is, what answer that you can expect him to listen to – while common soldiers risk their lives for two and sixpence a day, and fat women ride about in Rolls-Royce cars, nursing pekineses?

It is quite likely that this war will last three years. It will mean cruel overwork, cold dull winters, uninteresting food, lack of amusements, prolonged bombing. It cannot but lower the general standard of living, because the essential act of war is to manufacture armaments instead of consumable goods. The working class will have to suffer terrible things. And they *will* suffer them, almost indefinitely, provided that they know what they are fighting for. They are not cowards, and they are not even internationally minded. They can stand all that the Spanish workers stood, and more. But they will want some kind of proof that a better life is ahead for themselves and their children. The one sure earnest of that is that when they are taxed and overworked they shall see that the rich are being hit even harder. And if the rich squeal audibly, so much the better.

We can bring these things about, if we really want to. It is not true that public opinion has no power in England. It never makes itself heard without achieving something; it has been responsible for most of the changes for the better during the past six months. But we have moved with glacier-like slowness, and we have learned only from disasters. It took the fall of Paris to get rid of Chamberlain and the unnecessary suffering of scores of thousands of people in the East End to get rid or partially rid of Sir John Anderson. It is not worth losing a battle in order to bury a corpse. For we are fighting against swift evil intelligences, and time presses, and

> *history to the defeated*
> *May say Alas! but cannot alter or pardon.*

III

During the last six months there has been much talk of 'the Fifth Column'. From time to time obscure lunatics have been jailed for making speeches in favour of Hitler, and large numbers of German refugees have been interned, a thing which has almost certainly done us great harm in Europe. It is of course obvious that the idea of a large, organized army of Fifth Columnists suddenly appearing on the streets with weapons in their hands, as in Holland and Belgium, is ridiculous. Nevertheless a Fifth Column danger does exist. One can only consider it if one also considers in what way England might be defeated.

It does not seem probable that air bombing can settle a major war. England might well be invaded and conquered, but the invasion would be a dangerous gamble, and if it happened and failed it would probably leave us more united and less Blimp-ridden than before. Moreover, if England were overrun by foreign troops the English people would know that they had been beaten and would continue the struggle. It is doubtful whether they could be held down permanently, or whether Hitler wishes to keep an army of a million men stationed in these islands. A government of —, — and — (you can fill in the names) would suit him better. The English can probably not be bullied into surrender, but they might quite easily be bored, cajoled or cheated into it, provided that, as at Munich, they did not know that they were surrendering. It could happen most easily when the war seemed to be going well rather than badly. The threatening tone of so much of the German and Italian propaganda is a psychological mistake. It only gets home on intellectuals. With the general public the proper approach would be 'Let's call it a draw'. It is when a peace-offer along *those* lines is made that the pro-Fascists will raise their voices.

But who are the pro-Fascists? The idea of a Hitler victory appeals to the very rich, to the Communists, to Mosley's followers, to the pacifists, and to certain sections among the Catholics. Also, if things went badly enough on the Home Front, the whole of the poorer section of the working class might swing round to a position that was defeatist though not actively pro-Hitler.

In this motley list one can see the daring of German propaganda, its willingness to offer everything to everybody. But the various pro-Fascist forces are not consciously acting together, and they operate in different ways.

The Communists must certainly be regarded as pro-Hitler, and are bound to remain so unless Russian policy changes, but they have not very much influence. Mosley's Blackshirts, though now lying very low, are a more serious danger, because of the footing they probably possess in the armed forces. Still, even in its palmiest days Mosley's following can hardly have numbered 50,000. Pacifism is a psychological curiosity rather than a political movement. Some of the extremer pacifists, starting out with a complete renunciation of violence, have ended by warmly championing Hitler and even toying with antisemitism. This is interesting, but it is not important. 'Pure' pacifism, which is a by-product of naval power, can only appeal to people in very sheltered positions. Moreover, being negative and irresponsible, it does not inspire much devotion. Of the membership of the Peace Pledge Union, less than fifteen per cent even pay their annual subscriptions. None of these bodies of people, pacifists, Communists or Blackshirts, could bring a large-scale stop-the-war movement into being by their own efforts. But they might help to make things very much easier for a treacherous government negotiating surrender. Like the French Communists, they might become the half-conscious agents of millionaires.

The real danger is from above. One ought not to pay any attention to Hitler's recent line of talk about being the friend of the poor man, the enemy of plutocracy, etc. etc. Hitler's real self is in *Mein Kampf*, and in his actions. He has never persecuted the rich, except when they were Jews or when they tried actively to oppose him. He stands for a centralized economy which robs the capitalist of most of his power but leaves the structure of society much as before. The State controls industry, but there are still rich and poor, masters and men. Therefore, as against genuine Socialism, the moneyed class have always been on his side. This was crystal clear at the time of the Spanish Civil War, and clear again at the time when France surrendered. Hitler's puppet government are not working men, but a gang of bankers, gaga generals and corrupt right-wing politicians.

That kind of spectacular, *conscious* treachery is less likely to succeed in England, indeed is far less likely even to be tried. Nevertheless, to many payers of supertax this war is simply an insane family squabble which ought to be stopped at all costs. One need not doubt that a 'peace' movement is on foot somewhere in high places; probably a shadow Cabinet has already been formed. These people will get their chance not in the moment of defeat but in some stagnant period when boredom is reinforced by discontent. They will not talk about surrender, only about peace; and doubtless they will persuade themselves, and perhaps other people, that they are acting for the best. An army of unemployed led by millionaires quoting the Sermon on the Mount – that is our danger. But it cannot arise when we have once introduced a reasonable degree of social justice. The lady in the Rolls-Royce car is more damaging to morale than a fleet of Goering's bombing planes.

PART THREE:
The English Revolution

I

The English revolution started several years ago, and it began to gather momentum when the troops came back from Dunkirk. Like all else in England, it happens in a sleepy, unwilling way, but it is happening. The war has speeded it up, but it has also increased, and desperately, the necessity for speed.

Progress and reaction are ceasing to have anything to do with party labels. If one wishes to name a particular moment, one can say that the old distinction between Right and Left broke down when *Picture Post* was first published. What are the politics of *Picture Post*? Or of *Cavalcade*, or Priestley's broadcasts, or the leading articles in the *Evening Standard*? None of the old classifications will fit them. They merely point to the existence of multitudes of unlabelled people who have grasped within the last year or two that something is wrong. But since a classless, ownerless society is generally spoken of as 'Socialism', we can give that name to the society towards which we are now moving. The war and the revolution are inseparable. We cannot establish anything that a western nation would regard as Socialism without defeating Hitler; on the other hand we cannot defeat Hitler while we remain economically and socially in the nineteenth century. The past is fighting the future and we have two years, a year, possibly only a few months, to see to it that the future wins.

We cannot look to this or to any similar government to put through the necessary changes of its own accord. The initiative will have to come from below. That means that there will have to arise something that has never existed in England, a Socialist movement that actually has the mass of the people behind it. But one must start by recognizing why it is that English Socialism has failed.

In England there is only one Socialist party that has ever seriously mattered, the Labour Party. It has never been able to achieve any major change, because except in purely domestic matters it has never possessed a genuinely independent policy. It was and is primarily a party of the trade unions, devoted to raising wages and improving working conditions. This meant that all through the critical years it was directly interested in the prosperity of British capitalism. In particular it was interested in the maintenance of the British Empire, for the wealth of England was drawn largely from Asia and Africa. The standard of living of the trade-union workers, whom the Labour Party represented, depended indirectly on the sweating of Indian coolies. At the same time the Labour Party was a Socialist party, using Socialist phraseology, thinking in terms of an old-fashioned anti-imperialism and more or less pledged to make restitution to the coloured races. It had to stand for the 'independence' of India, just as it had to stand for disarmament and 'progress' generally. Nevertheless everyone was aware that this was nonsense. In the age of the tank and the bombing plane, backward agricultural countries like India and the African colonies can no more be independent than can a cat or a dog. Had any Labour government come into office with a clear majority and then proceeded to grant India anything that could truly be called independence, India would simply have been absorbed by Japan, or divided between Japan and Russia.

To a Labour government in power, three imperial policies would have been open. One was to continue administering the Empire exactly as before, which meant dropping all pretensions to Socialism. Another was to set the subject peoples 'free', which meant in practice handing them over to Japan, Italy and other predatory powers, and incidentally causing a catastrophic drop in the British standard of living. The third was to develop a *positive* imperial policy, and aim at transforming the Empire into a federation of Socialist states, like a looser and freer version of the Union of Soviet Republics. But the Labour Party's history and background made this impossible. It was a party of the trade unions, hopelessly parochial in outlook, with little interest in imperial affairs and no contacts among the men who actually held the Empire together. It would have had to hand the administration of India and Africa and the whole job of imperial defence to men drawn from a different class and traditionally hostile to Socialism. Overshadowing everything was the doubt whether a Labour government which meant business could make itself obeyed. For all the size of its following, the Labour Party had no footing in the navy, little or none in the army or air force, none whatever in the Colonial Services, and not even a sure footing in the Home Civil Service. In England its position was strong but not unchallengeable, and outside England all the points were in the hands of its enemies. Once in power, the same dilemma would always have faced it: carry out your promise, and risk revolt, or continue with the same policy as the Conservatives, and stop talking about Socialism. The Labour leaders never found a solution, and from 1935 onwards it was very doubtful whether they had any wish to take office. They had degenerated into a Permanent Opposition.

Outside the Labour Party there existed several extremist parties, of whom the Communists were the strongest. The Communists had considerable influence in the Labour Party in the years 1920-26 and 1935-9. Their chief importance, and that of the whole left wing of the Labour movement, was the part they played in alienating the middle classes from Socialism.

The history of the past seven years has made it perfectly clear that Communism has no chance in western Europe. The appeal of Fascism is enormously greater. In one country after another the Communists have been rooted out by their more up-to-date enemies, the Nazis. In the English-speaking countries they never had a serious footing. The creed they were spreading could appeal only to a rather rare type of person, found chiefly in the middle-class intelligentsia, the type who has ceased to love his own country but still feels the need of patriotism, and therefore develops patriotic sentiments towards Russia. By 1940, after working for twenty years and spending a great deal of money, the British Communists had barely 20,000 members, actually a smaller number than they had started out with in 1920. The other Marxist parties were of even less importance. They had not the Russian money and prestige behind them, and even more than the Communists they were tied to the nineteenth-century doctrine of the class war. They continued year after year to preach this out-of-date gospel, and never drew any inference from the fact that it got them no followers.

Nor did any strong native Fascist movement grow up.

Material conditions were not bad enough, and no leader who could be taken seriously was forthcoming. One would have had to look a long time to find a man more barren of ideas than Sir Oswald Mosley. He was as hollow as a jug. Even the elementary fact that Fascism must not offend national sentiment had escaped him. His entire movement was imitated slavishly from abroad, the uniform and the party programme from Italy and the salute from Germany, with the Jew-baiting tacked on as an afterthought, Mosley having actually started his movement with Jews among his most prominent followers. A man of the stamp of Bottomley or Lloyd George could perhaps have brought a real British Fascist movement into existence. But such leaders only appear when the psychological need for them exists.

After twenty years of stagnation and unemployment, the entire English Socialist movement was unable to produce a version of Socialism which the mass of the people could even find desirable. The Labour Party stood for a timid reformism, the Marxists were looking at the modern world through nineteenth-century spectacles. Both ignored agriculture and imperial problems, and both antagonized the middle classes. The suffocating stupidity of left-wing propaganda had frightened away whole classes of necessary people, factory managers, airmen, naval officers, farmers, white-collar workers, shopkeepers, policemen. All of these people had been taught to think of Socialism as something which menaced their livelihood, or as something seditious, alien, 'anti-British' as they would have called it. Only the intellectuals, the least useful section of the middle class, gravitated towards the movement.

A Socialist Party which genuinely wished to achieve anything would have started by facing several facts which to this day are considered unmentionable in left-wing circles. It would have recognized that England is more united than most countries, that the British workers have a great deal to lose besides their chains, and that the differences in outlook and habits between class and class are rapidly diminishing. In general, it would have recognized that the old-fashioned 'proletarian revolution' is an impossibility. But all through the between-war years no Socialist programme that was both revolutionary and workable ever appeared; basically, no doubt, because no one genuinely wanted any major change to happen. The Labour leaders wanted to go on and on, drawing their salaries and periodically swapping jobs with the Conservatives. The Communists wanted to go on and on, suffering a comfortable martyrdom, meeting with endless defeats and afterwards putting the blame on other people. The left-wing intelligentsia wanted to go on and on, sniggering at the Blimps, sapping away at middle-class morale, but still keeping their favoured position as hangers-on of the dividend-drawers. Labour Party politics had become a variant of Conservatism, 'revolutionary' politics had become a game of make-believe.

Now, however, the circumstances have changed, the drowsy years have ended. Being a Socialist no longer means kicking theoretically against a system which in practice you are fairly well satisfied with. This time our predicament is real. It is 'the Philistines be upon thee, Samson'. We have got to make our words take physical shape, or perish. We know very well that with its present social structure England cannot survive, and we have got to make other people see that fact and act upon it. We cannot win the war without introducing Socialism, nor establish Socialism without winning the war. At such a time it is possible, as it was not in the peaceful years, to be both revolutionary and realistic. A Socialist movement which can swing the mass of the people behind it, drive the pro-Fascists out of positions of control, wipe out the grosser injustices and let the working class see that they have something to fight for, win over the middle classes instead of antagonizing them, produce a workable imperial policy instead of a mixture of humbug and Utopianism, bring patriotism and intelligence into partnership – for the first time, a movement of such a kind becomes possible.

II

The fact that we are at war has turned Socialism from a textbook word into a realizable policy.

The inefficiency of private capitalism has been proved all over Europe. Its injustice has been proved in the East End of London. Patriotism, against which the Socialists fought so long, has become a tremendous lever in their hands. People who at any other time would cling like glue to their miserable scraps of privilege, will surrender them fast enough when their country is in danger. War is the greatest of all agents of change. It speeds up all processes, wipes out minor distinctions, bring realities to the surface. Above all, war brings it home to the individual that he is *not* altogether an individual. It is only because they are aware of this that men will die on the field of battle. At this moment it is not so much a question of surrendering life as of surrendering leisure, comfort, economic liberty, social prestige. There are very few people in England who really want to see their country conquered by Germany. If it can be made clear that defeating Hitler means wiping out class privilege, the great mass of middling people, the £6 a week to £2,000 a year class, will probably be on our side. These people are quite indispensable, because they include most of the technical experts. Obviously the snobbishness and political ignorance of people like airmen and naval officers will be a very great difficulty. But without those airmen, destroyer commanders, etc. etc. we could not survive for a week. The only approach to them is through their patriotism. An intelligent Socialist movement will *use* their patriotism, instead of merely insulting it, as hitherto.

But do I mean that there will be no opposition? Of course not. It would be childish to expect anything of the kind.

There will be a bitter political struggle, and there will be unconscious and half-conscious sabotage everywhere. At some point or other it may be necessary to use violence. It is easy to imagine a pro-Fascist rebellion breaking out in, for instance, India. We shall have to fight against bribery, ignorance and snobbery. The bankers and the larger businessmen, the landowners and dividend-drawers, the officials with their prehensile bottoms, will obstruct for all they are worth. Even the middle classes will writhe when their accustomed way of life is menaced. But just because the English sense of national unity has never disintegrated, because patriotism is finally stronger then class-hatred, the chances are that the will of the majority will prevail. It is no use imagining that one can make fundamental changes without causing a split in the nation; but the treacherous minority will be far smaller in time of war than it would be at any other time.

The swing of opinion is visibly happening, but it cannot be counted on to happen fast enough of its own accord. This war is a race between the consolidation of Hitler's empire and the growth of democratic consciousness. Everywhere in England you can see a ding-dong battle raging to and fro – in Parliament and in the Government, in the factories and the armed forces, in the pubs and air-raid shelters, in the newspapers and on the radio. Every day there are tiny defeats, tiny victories. Morrison for Home Secretary – a few yards forward. Priestley shoved off the air – a few yards back. It is a struggle between the groping and the unteachable, between the young and the old, between the living and the dead. But it is very necessary that the discontent which undoubtedly exists should take a purposeful and not merely obstructive form. It is time for *the people* to define their war aims. What is wanted is a simple, concrete programme of action, which can be given all possible publicity, and round which public opinion can group itself.

I suggest that the following six-point programme is the kind of thing we need. The first three points deal with England's internal policy, the other three with the Empire and the world:

1. Nationalization of land, mines, railways, banks and major industries.

2. Limitation of incomes, on such a scale that the highest tax-free income in Britain does not exceed the lowest by more than ten to one.

3. Reform of the educational system along democratic lines.

4. Immediate Dominion status for India, with power to secede when the war is over.

5. Formation of an Imperial General Council, in which the coloured peoples are to be represented.

6. Declaration of formal alliance with China, Abyssinia and all other victims of the Fascist powers.

The general tendency of this programme is unmistakable. It aims quite frankly at turning this war into a revolutionary war and England into a Socialist democracy. I have deliberately included in it nothing that the simplest person could not understand and see the reason for. In the form in which I have put it, it could be printed on the front page of the *Daily Mirror*. But for the purposes of this book a certain amount of amplification is needed.

1. *Nationalization*. One can 'nationalize' industry by the stroke of a pen, but the actual process is slow and complicated. What is needed is that the ownership of all major industry shall be formally vested in the State, representing the common people. Once that is done it becomes possible to eliminate the class of mere *owners* who live not by virtue of anything they produce but by the possession of title-deeds and share certificates. State-ownership implies, therefore, that nobody shall live without working. How sudden a change in the conduct of industry it implies is less certain. In a country like England we cannot rip down the whole structure and build again from the bottom, least of all in time of war. Inevitably the majority of industrial concerns will continue with much the same personnel as before, the one-time owners or managing directors carrying on with their jobs as State employees. There is reason to think that many of the smaller capitalists would actually welcome some such arrangement. The resistance will come from the big capitalists, the bankers, the landlords and the idle rich, roughly speaking the class with over £2,000 a year – and even if one counts in all their dependants there are not more than half a million of these people in England. Nationalization of agricultural land implies cutting out the landlord and the tithe drawer, but not necessarily interfering with the farmer. It is difficult to imagine any reorganization of English agriculture that would not retain most of the existing farms as units, at any rate at the beginning. The farmer, when he is

competent, will continue as a salaried manager. He is virtually that already, with the added disadvantage of having to make a profit and being permanently in debt to the bank. With certain kinds of petty trading, and even the small-scale ownership of land, the State will probably not interfere at all. It would be a great mistake to start by victimizing the smallholder class, for instance. These people are necessary, on the whole they are competent, and the amount of work they do depends on the feeling that they are 'their own masters'. But the State will certainly impose an upward limit to the ownership of land (probably fifteen acres at the very most), and will never permit any ownership of land in town areas.

From the moment that all productive goods have been declared the property of the State, the common people will feel, as they cannot feel now, that the State *is themselves*. They will be ready then to endure the sacrifices that are ahead of us, war or no war. And even if the face of England hardly seems to change, on the day that our main industries are formally nationalized the dominance of a single class will have been broken. From then onwards the emphasis will be shifted from ownership to management, from privilege to competence. It is quite possible that State-ownership will in itself bring about less social change than will be forced upon us by the common hardships of war. But it is the necessary first step without which any *real* reconstruction is impossible.

2. *Incomes*. Limitation of incomes implies the fixing of a minimum wage, which implies a managed internal currency based simply on the amount of consumption goods available. And this again implies a stricter rationing scheme than is now in operation. It is no use at this stage of the world's history to suggest that all human beings should have *exactly* equal incomes. It has been shown over and over again that without

some kind of money reward there is no incentive to undertake certain jobs. On the other hand the money reward need not be very large. In practice it is impossible that earnings should be limited quite as rigidly as I have suggested. There will always be anomalies and evasions. But there is no reason why ten to one should not be the maximum normal variation. And within those limits some sense of equality is possible. A man with £3 a week and a man with £1,500 a year can feel themselves fellow creatures, which the Duke of Westminster and the sleepers on the Embankment benches cannot.

3. *Education.* In wartime, educational reform must necessarily be promise rather than performance. At the moment we are not in a position to raise the school-leaving age or increase the teaching staffs of the elementary schools. But there are certain immediate steps that we could take towards a democratic educational system. We could start by abolishing the autonomy of the public schools and the older universities and flooding them with State-aided pupils chosen simply on grounds of ability. At present, public-school education is partly a training in class prejudice and partly a sort of tax that the middle classes pay to the upper class in return for the right to enter certain professions. It is true that that state of affairs is altering. The middle classes have begun to rebel against the expensiveness of education, and the war will bankrupt the majority of the public schools if it continues for another year or two. The evacuation is also producing certain minor changes. But there is a danger that some of the older schools, which will be able to weather the financial storm longest, will survive in some form or another as festering centres of snobbery. As for the 10,000 'private' schools that England possesses, the vast majority of them deserve nothing except suppression. They are simply commercial undertak-

ings, and in many cases their educational level is actually lower than that of the elementary schools. They merely exist because of a widespread idea that there is something disgraceful in being educated by the public authorities. The State could quell this idea by declaring itself responsible for *all* education, even if at the start this were no more than a gesture. We need gestures as well as actions. It is all too obvious that our talk of 'defending democracy' is nonsense while it is a mere accident of birth that decides whether a gifted child shall or shall not get the education it deserves.

4. *India*. What we must offer India is not 'freedom', which, as I have said earlier, is impossible, but alliance, partnership – in a word, equality. But we must also tell the Indians that they are free to secede, if they want to. Without that there can be no equality of partnership, and our claim to be defending the coloured peoples against Fascism will never be believed. But it is a mistake to imagine that if the Indians were free to cut themselves adrift they would immediately do so. When a British government *offers* them unconditional independence, they will refuse it. For as soon as they have the power to secede the chief reasons for doing so will have disappeared.

A complete severance of the two countries would be a disaster for India no less than for England. Intelligent Indians know this. As things are at present, India not only cannot defend itself, it is hardly even capable of feeding itself. The whole administration of the country depends on a framework of experts (engineers, forest officers, railwaymen, soldiers, doctors) who are predominantly English and could not be replaced within five or ten years. Moreover, English is the chief lingua franca and nearly the whole of the Indian intelligentsia is deeply anglicized. Any transference to foreign rule – for if the British marched out of India the Japanese and other powers would immediately march in – would mean an immense dislocation. Neither the Japanese, the Russians, the Germans nor the Italians would be capable of administering India even at the low level of efficiency that is attained by the British. They do not possess the necessary supplies of technical experts or the knowledge of languages and local conditions and they probably could not win the confidence of indispensable go-betweens such as the Eurasians. If India were simply 'liberated', i.e. deprived of British military protection, the first result would be a fresh foreign conquest, and the second a series of enormous famines which would kill millions of people within a few years.

What India needs is the power to work out its own constitution without British interference, but in some kind of partnership that ensures its military protection and technical advice. This is unthinkable until there is a Socialist government in England. For at least eighty years England has artificially prevented the development of India, partly from fear of trade competition if Indian industries were too highly developed, partly bacause backward peoples are more easily governed than civilized ones. It is a commonplace that the average Indian suffers far more from his own countrymen than from the British. The petty Indian capitalist exploits the town worker with the utmost ruthlessness, the peasant lives from birth to death in the grip of the money-lender. But all this is an indirect result of the British rule, which aims half-consciously at keeping India as backward as possible. The classes most loyal to Britain are the princes, the landowners and the business community – in general, the reactionary classes who are doing fairly well out of the *status quo*. The moment that England ceased to stand towards India in the relation of an exploiter, the balance of forces would be altered.

No need then for the British to flatter the ridiculous Indian princes, with their gilded elephants and cardboard armies, to prevent the growth of the Indian trade unions, to play off Moslem against Hindu, to protect the worthless life of the money-lender, to receive the salaams of toadying minor officials, to prefer the half-barbarous Gurkha to the educated Bengali. Once check that stream of dividends that flows from the bodies of Indian coolies to the banking accounts of old ladies in Cheltenham, and the whole sahib–native nexus, with its haughty ignorance on one side and envy and servility on the other, can come to an end. Englishmen and Indians can work side by side for the development of India, and for the training of Indians in all the arts which, so far, they have been systematically prevented from learning. How many of the existing British personnel in India, commercial or official, would fall in with such an arrangement – which would mean ceasing once and for all to be 'sahibs' – is a different question. But, broadly speaking, more is to be hoped from the younger men and from those officials (civil engineers, forestry and agriculture experts, doctors, educationists) who have been scientifically educated. The higher officials, the provincial governors, commissioners, judges, etc. are hopeless; but they are also the most easily replaceable.

That, roughly, is what would be meant by Dominion status if it were offered to India by a Socialist government. It is an offer of partnership on equal terms until such time as the world has ceased to be ruled by bombing planes. But we must add to it the unconditional right to secede. It is the only way of proving that we mean what we say. And what applies to India applies, *mutatis mutandis*, to Burma, Malaya and most of our African possessions.

5 and 6 explain themselves. They are the necessary pre-

liminary to any claim that we are fighting this war for the protection of peaceful peoples against Fascist aggression.

Is it impossibly hopeful to think that such a policy as this could get a following in England? A year ago, even six months ago, it would have been, but not now. Moreover – and this is the peculiar opportunity of this moment – it could be given the necessary publicity. There is now a considerable weekly press, with a circulation of millions, which would be ready to popularize – if not *exactly* the programme I have sketched above, at any rate *some* policy along those lines. There are even three or four daily papers which would be prepared to give it a sympathetic hearing. That is the distance we have travelled in the last six months.

But is such a policy realizable? That depends entirely on ourselves.

Some of the points I have suggested are of the kind that could be carried out immediately, others would take years or decades and even then would not be perfectly achieved. No political programme is ever carried out in its entirety. But what matters is that that or something like it should be our declared policy. It is always the *direction* that counts. It is of course quite hopeless to expect the present Government to pledge itself to any policy that implies turning this war into a revolutionary war. It is at best a government of compromise, with Churchill riding two horses like a circus acrobat. Before such measures as limitation of incomes become even thinkable, there will have to be a complete shift of power away from the old ruling class. If during this winter the war settles into another stagnant period, we ought in my opinion to agitate for a General Election, a thing which the Tory Party machine will make frantic efforts to prevent. But even without an election we can get the government we want, provided that we want it urgently enough. A real shove from below will accomplish it. As to who will be in that government when it comes, I make no guess. I only know that the right men will be there when the people really want them, for it is movements that make leaders and not leaders movements.

Within a year, perhaps even within six months, if we are still unconquered, we shall see the rise of something that has never existed before, a specifically *English* Socialist movement. Hitherto there has been only the Labour Party, which was the creation of the working class but did not aim at any fundamental change, and Marxism, which was a German theory interpreted by Russians and unsuccessfully transplanted to England. There was nothing that really touched the heart of the English people. Throughout its entire history the English Socialist movement has never produced a song with a catchy tune – nothing like *La Marseillaise* or *La Cucuracha*, for instance. When a Socialist movement native to England appears, the Marxists, like all others with a vested interest in the past, will be its bitter enemies. Inevitably they will denounce it as 'Fascism'. Already it is customary among the more soft-boiled intellectuals of the Left to declare that if we fight against the Nazis we shall 'go Nazi' ourselves. They might almost equally well say that if we fight Negroes we shall turn black. To 'go Nazi' we should have to have the history of Germany behind us. Nations do not escape from their past merely by making a revolution. An English Socialist government will transform the nation from top to bottom, but it will still bear all over it the unmistakable marks of our own civilization, the peculiar civilization which I discussed earlier in this book.

It will not be doctrinaire, nor even logical. It will abolish the House of Lords, but quite probably will not abolish the

Monarchy. It will leave anachronisms and loose ends everywhere, the judge in his ridiculous horsehair wig and the lion and the unicorn on the soldier's cap-buttons. It will not set up any explicit class dictatorship. It will group itself round the old Labour Party and its mass following will be in the trade unions, but it will draw into it most of the middle class and many of the younger sons of the bourgeoisie. Most of its directing brains will come from the new indeterminate class of skilled workers, technical experts, airmen, scientists, architects and journalists, the people who feel at home in the radio and ferro-concrete age. But it will never lose touch with the tradition of compromise and the belief in a law that is above the State. It will shoot traitors, but it will give them a solemn trial beforehand and occasionally it will acquit them. It will crush any open revolt promptly and cruelly, but it will interfere very little with the spoken and written word. Political parties with different names will still exist, revolutionary sects will still be publishing their newspapers and making as little impression as ever. It will disestablish the Church, but will not persecute religion. It will retain a vague reverence for the Christian moral code, and from time to time will refer to England as 'a Christian country'. The Catholic Church will war against it, but the Nonconformist sects and the bulk of the Anglican Church will be able to come to terms with it. It will show a power of assimilating the past which will shock foreign observers and sometimes make them doubt whether any revolution has happened.

But all the same it will have done the essential thing. It will have nationalized industry, scaled down incomes, set up a classless educational system. Its real nature will be apparent from the hatred which the surviving rich men of the world will feel for it. It will aim not at disintegrating the Empire but at turning it into a federation of Socialist states, freed not so much from the British flag as from the money-lender, the dividend-drawer and the wooden-headed British official. Its war strategy will be totally different from that of any property-ruled state, because it will not be afraid of the revolutionary after-effects when any existing régime is brought down. It will not have the smallest scruple about attacking hostile neutrals or stirring up native rebellion in enemy colonies. It will fight in such a way that even if it is beaten its memory will be dangerous to the victor, as the memory of the French Revolution was dangerous to Metternich's Europe. The dictators will fear it as they could not fear the existing British régime, even if its military strength were ten times what it is.

But at this moment, when the drowsy life of England has barely altered, and the offensive contrast of wealth and poverty still exists everywhere, even amid the bombs, why do I dare to say that all these things 'will' happen?

Because the time has come when one can predict the future in terms of an 'either – or'. Either we turn this war into a revolutionary war (I do not say that our policy will be *exactly* what I have indicated above – merely that it will be along those general lines) or we lose it, and much more besides. Quite soon it will be possible to say definitely that our feet are set upon one path or the other. But at any rate it is certain that with our present social structure we cannot win. Our real forces, physical, moral or intellectual, cannot be mobilized.

III

Patriotism has nothing to do with Conservatism. It is actually the opposite of Conservatism, since it is a devotion to something that is always changing and yet is felt to be mystically the same. It is the bridge between the future and the past. No real revolutionary has ever been an internationalist.

During the past twenty years the negative, *fainéant* outlook which has been fashionable among English left-wingers, the sniggering of the intellectuals at patriotism and physical courage, the persistent effort to chip away English morale and spread a hedonistic, what-do-I-get-out-of-it attitude to life, has done nothing but harm. It would have been harmful even if we had been living in the squashy League of Nations universe that these people imagined. In an age of fuehrers and bombing planes it was a disaster. However little we may like it, toughness is the price of survival. A nation trained to think hedonistically cannot survive amid peoples who work like slaves and breed like rabbits, and whose chief national industry is war. English Socialists of nearly all colours wanted to make a stand against Fascism, but at the same time they have aimed at making their own countrymen unwarlike. They have failed, because in England traditional loyalties are stronger than new ones. But in spite of all the 'anti-Fascist' heroics of the left-wing press, what chance should we have stood when the real struggle with Fascism came, if the average Englishman had been the kind of creature that the *New Statesman*, the *Daily Worker* or even the *News Chronicle* wished to make him?

Up to 1935 virtually all English left-wingers were vaguely pacifist. After 1935 the more vocal of them flung themselves eagerly into the Popular Front movement, which was simply an evasion of the whole problem posed by Fascism. It set out to be 'anti-Fascist' in a purely negative way – 'against' Fascism without being 'for' any discoverable policy – and underneath it lay the flabby idea that when the time came the Russians would do our fighting for us. It is astonishing how this illusion fails to die. Every week sees its spate of letters to the press, pointing out that if we had a government with no Tories in it the Russians could hardly avoid coming round to our side. Or we are to publish high-sounding war aims (*vide* books like *Unser Kampf*, *A Hundred Million Allies – If We Chose*, etc.), whereupon the European populations will infallibly rise on our behalf. It is the same idea all the time – look abroad for your inspiration, get someone else to do your fighting for you. Underneath it lies the frightful inferiority complex of the English intellectual, the belief that the English are no longer a martial race, no longer capable of enduring.

In truth there is no reason to think that anyone will do our fighting for us yet awhile, except the Chinese, who have been doing it for three years already.[3] The Russians may be driven to fight on our side by the fact of a direct attack, but they have made it clear enough that they will not stand up to the German army if there is any way of avoiding it. In any case they are not likely to be attracted by the spectacle of a left-wing government in England. The present Russian régime must almost certainly be hostile to any revolution in the West. The subject peoples of Europe will rebel when Hitler begins to totter, but not earlier. Our potential allies are not the Europeans but on the one hand the Americans, who will need a year to mobilize their resources even if Big Business can be brought to heel, and on the other hand the coloured peoples, who cannot be even sentimentally on our side till our own revolution has started. For a long time, a year, two years, possibly three years, England has got to be the shock-absorber of the world. We have got to face bombing, hunger, overwork, influenza, boredom and treacherous peace offers. Manifestly it is a time to stiffen morale, not to weaken it. Instead of taking the mechanically anti-British attitude which is usual on the Left, it is better to consider what the world would really be like if the English-speaking culture perished. For it is childish to suppose that the other English-speaking countries, even the U.S.A., will be unaffected if Britain is conquered.

Lord Halifax, and all his tribe, believe that when the war is over things will be exactly as they were before. Back to the crazy pavement of Versailles, back to 'democracy', i.e. capitalism, back to dole queues and the Rolls-Royce cars, back to the grey top hats and the sponge-bag trousers, *in saecula saeculorum*. It is of course obvious that nothing of the kind is going to happen. A feeble imitation of it might just possibly happen in the case of a negotiated peace, but only for a short while.

3. Written before the outbreak of the war in Greece. [Author's footnote.]

Laissez-faire capitalism is dead.[4] The choice lies between the kind of collective society that Hitler will set up and the kind that can arise if he is defeated.

If Hitler wins this war he will consolidate his rule over Europe, Africa and the Middle East, and if his armies have not been too greatly exhausted beforehand, he will wrench vast territories from Soviet Russia. He will set up a graded caste-society in which the German *Herrenvolk* ('master race' or 'aristocratic race') will rule over Slavs and other lesser peoples whose job it will be to produce low-priced agricultural products. He will reduce the coloured peoples once and for all to outright slavery. The real quarrel of the Fascist powers with British imperialism is that they know that it is disintegrating. Another twenty years along the present line of development, and India will be a peasant republic linked with England only by voluntary alliance. The 'semi-apes' of whom Hitler speaks with such loathing will be flying aeroplanes and manufacturing machine-guns. The Fascist dream of a slave empire will be at an end. On the other hand, if we are defeated we simply hand over our own victims to new masters who come fresh to the job and have not developed any scruples.

But more is involved than the fate of the coloured peoples. Two incompatible visions of life are fighting one another. 'Between democracy and totalitarianism,' says Mussolini, 'there can be no compromise.' The two creeds cannot even, for any length of time, live side by side. So long as democracy exists, even in its very imperfect English form, totalitarianism is in deadly danger. The whole English-speaking world is haunted by the idea of human equality, and though it would

---

4. It is interesting to notice that Mr Kennedy, U.S.A. Ambassador in London, remarked on his return to New York in October 1940 that as a result of the war 'democracy is finished'. By 'democracy', of course, he meant private capitalism. [Author's footnote.]

be simply a lie to say that either we or the Americans have ever acted up to our professions, still, the *idea* is there, and it is capable of one day becoming a reality. From the English-speaking culture, if it does not perish, a society of free and equal human beings will ultimately arise. But it is precisely the idea of human equality – the 'Jewish' or 'Judaeo-Christian' idea of equality – that Hitler came into the world to destroy. He has, heaven knows, said so often enough. The thought of a world in which black men would be as good as white men and Jews treated as human beings brings him the same horror and despair as the thought of endless slavery brings to us.

It is important to keep in mind how irreconcilable these two viewpoints are. Some time within the next year a pro-Hitler reaction within the left-wing intelligentsia is likely enough. There are premonitory signs of it already. Hitler's positive achievement appeals to the emptiness of these people, and, in the case of those with pacifist leanings, to their masochism. One knows in advance more or less what they will say. They will start by refusing to admit that British capitalism is evolving into something different, or that the defeat of Hitler can mean any more than a victory for the British and American millionaires. And from that they will proceed to argue that, after all, democracy is 'just the same as' or 'just as bad as' totalitarianism. There is *not much* freedom of speech in England; therefore there is *no more* than exists in Germany. To be on the dole is a horrible experience; therefore it is *no worse* to be in the torture-chambers of the Gestapo. In general, two blacks make a white, half a loaf is the same as no bread.

But in reality, whatever may be true about democracy and totalitarianism, it is not true that they are the same. It would not be true, even if British democracy were incapable of evolving beyond its present stage. The whole conception of the militarized continental state, with its secret police, its censored literature and its conscript labour, is utterly different from that of the loose maritime democracy, with its slums and unemployment, its strikes and party politics. It is the difference between land power and sea power, between cruelty and inefficiency, between lying and self-deception, between the S.S. man and the rent-collector. And in choosing between them one chooses not so much on the strength of what they now are as of what they are capable of becoming. But in a sense it is irrelevant whether democracy, at its highest or at its lowest, is 'better' than totalitarianism. To decide that one would have to have access to absolute standards. The only question that matters is where one's real sympathies will lie when the pinch comes. The intellectuals who are so fond of balancing democracy against totalitarianism and 'proving' that one is as bad as the other are simply frivolous people who have never been shoved up against realities. They show the same shallow misunderstanding of Fascism now, when they are beginning to flirt with it, as a year or two ago, when they were squealing against it. The question is not, 'Can you make out a debating-society "case" in favour of Hitler?' The question is, 'Do you genuinely accept that case? Are you willing to submit to Hitler's rule? Do you want to see England conquered, or don't you?' It would be better to be sure on that point before frivolously siding with the enemy. For there is no such thing as neutrality in war; in practice one must help one side or the other.

When the pinch comes, no one bred in the western tradition can accept the Fascist vision of life. It is important to realize that *now*, and to grasp what it entails. With all its sloth, hypocrisy and injustice, the English-speaking civilization is the only large obstacle in Hitler's path. It is a living contradiction of all the 'infallible' dogmas of Fascism. That is why all Fascist writers for years past have agreed that England's power must be destroyed. England must be 'exterminated', must be 'annihilated', must 'cease to exist'. Strategically it would be possible for this war to end with Hitler in secure possession of Europe, and with the British Empire intact and British sea-power barely affected. But ideologically it is not possible; were Hitler to make an offer along those lines, it could only be treacherously, with a view to conquering England indirectly or renewing the attack at some more favourable moment. England cannot possibly be allowed to remain as a sort of funnel through which deadly ideas from beyond the Atlantic flow into the police states of Europe. And turning it round to our point of view, we see the vastness of the issue before us, the all-importance of preserving our democracy more or less as we have known it. But to *preserve* is always to *extend*. The choice before us is not so much between victory and defeat as between revolution and apathy. If the thing we are fighting for is altogether destroyed, it will have been destroyed partly by our own act.

It could happen that England could introduce the beginnings of Socialism, turn this war into a revolutionary war, and still be defeated. That is at any rate thinkable. But, terrible as it would be for anyone who is now adult, it would be far less deadly than the 'compromise peace' which a few rich men and their hired liars are hoping for. The final ruin of England could only be accomplished by an English government acting under orders from Berlin. But that cannot happen if England has awakened beforehand. For in that case the defeat would be unmistakable, the struggle would continue, the *idea* would survive. The difference between going down fighting, and surrendering without a fight, is by no means a question of 'honour' and schoolboy heroics. Hitler said once that to *accept* defeat destroys the soul of a nation. This sounds like a piece of claptrap, but it is strictly true. The defeat of 1870 did not lessen the world-influence of France. The Third Republic had more influence, intellectually, than the France of Napoleon III. But the sort of peace that Pétain, Laval and Co. have accepted can only be purchased by deliberately wiping out the national culture. The Vichy Government will enjoy a spurious independence only on condition that it destroys the distinctive marks of French culture: republicanism, secularism, respect for the intellect, absence of colour prejudice. We cannot be *utterly* defeated if we have made our revolution beforehand. We may see German troops marching down Whitehall, but another process, ultimately deadly to the German power-dream, will have been started. The Spanish people were defeated, but the things they learned during those two and a half memorable years will one day come back upon the Spanish Fascists like a boomerang.

A piece of Shakespearean bombast was much quoted at the beginning of the war. Even Mr Chamberlain quoted it once, if my memory does not deceive me:

> *Come the four corners of the world in arms*
> *And we shall shock them: naught shall make us rue*
> *If England to herself do rest but true.*

It is right enough, if you interpret it rightly. But England has got to be true to herself. She is not being true to herself while the refugees who have sought our shores are penned up in concentration camps, and company directors work out subtle schemes to dodge their Excess Profits Tax. It is goodbye to the *Tatler* and the *Bystander*, and farewell to the lady in the Rolls-Royce car. The heirs of Nelson and of Cromwell are not in the House of Lords. They are in the fields and the streets, in the factories and the armed forces, in the four-ale bar and the suburban back garden; and at present they are still kept under by a generation of ghosts. Compared with the task of bringing the real England to the surface, even the winning of the war, necessary though it is, is secondary. By revolution we become more ourselves, not less. There is no question of stopping short, striking a compromise, salvaging 'democracy', standing still. Nothing ever stands still. We must add to our heritage or lose it, we must grow greater or grow less, we must go forward or backward. I believe in England, and I believe that we shall go forward.

MORE ABOUT PENGUINS, PELICANS, PEREGRINES AND PUFFINS

For further information about books available from Penguins please write to Dept EP, Penguin Books Ltd, Harmondsworth, Middlesex UB7 0DA.

In the U.S.A.: For a complete list of books available from Penguins in the United States write to Dept DG, Penguin Books, 299 Murray Hill Parkway, East Rutherford, New Jersey 07073.

In Canada: For a complete list of books available from Penguins in Canada write to Penguin Books Canada Ltd, 2801 John Street, Markham, Ontario L3R 1B4.

In Australia: For a complete list of books available from Penguins in Australia write to the Marketing Department, Penguin Books Australia Ltd, P.O. Box 257, Ringwood, Victoria 3134.

In New Zealand: For a complete list of books available from Penguins in New Zealand write to the Marketing Department, Penguin Books (N.Z.) Ltd, Private Bag, Takapuna, Auckland 9.

In India: For a complete list of books available from Penguins in India write to Penguin Overseas Ltd, 706 Eros Apartments, 56 Nehru Place, New Delhi 110019.

A celebrated biography in Penguins

GEORGE ORWELL: A LIFE
Bernard Crick

'A triumph of the first order' – Michael Foot in the *New Standard*

'It is hardly worth using up space to declare just how good it is. Different readers will come away from its seventeen pungent and packed chapters with diverse memories of its excellence' – Peter Sedgwick in the *Guardian*

'Crick has a remarkably independent mind and a large, irascible way of seeing things' – Noel Annan in the *New York Review of Books*

'Crick's analytical mind, combined with his mastery of the historical background and context, make him the ideal guide' – Arthur Koestler in the *Observer*

'Assured and eloquent . . . In its own uncompromised integrity it is both monumental and appealing' – *Los Angeles Times*

Winner of the 1980 Yorkshire Post Book of the Year Award

George Orwell

ANIMAL FARM

In this searing satire upon dictatorship George Orwell, who has been compared to Swift, tells the story of a revolution that went wrong. The animals on a farm, led by the pigs, drive out their master and take over the farm. But the purity of their original doctrine is soon perverted.

'A very amusing and intrinsically wise book' – *Guardian*

NINETEEN EIGHTY-FOUR

1984 is the year in which it happens. The world is divided into three great powers, Oceania, Eurasia, and Eastasia, each perpetually at war with one another. Throughout Oceania 'The Party' rules through the agency of all-powerful ministries. The authorities use every device to keep a check on the people's thoughts, words, and deeds. Against this nightmare background is played out the drama of Winston Smith, who rebelled against the Party's rule.

Also published:

BURMESE DAYS
A CLERGYMAN'S DAUGHTER
THE DECLINE OF THE ENGLISH
MURDER AND OTHER ESSAYS
INSIDE THE WHALE AND OTHER STORIES

Also by George Orwell in Penguins

DOWN AND OUT IN PARIS AND LONDON

After an Etonian education and service in the Imperial Police, George Orwell embarked on his first attempt to confront the world of poverty and failure, to defy the money values of the predatory world and of his own privileged background. In Paris and in London, working as a *plongeur* or spending nights with the tramps in the 'spike', Orwell mingled with the victims of modern society to produce this vivid account of the first steps on the road that led him to Wigan Pier and Catalonia.

DECLINE OF THE ENGLISH MURDER AND OTHER ESSAYS

A collection of some of the less accessible essays by the author of *Animal Farm*. Including his lament for the inferior quality of modern murders and his comments on the changing face of fictional crime; his long essay on Dickens; and his shrewd critical remarks on Kipling and on the peculiar genius of Salvador Dali; eyewitness accounts of a hanging in Burma and a lazar-house in Paris; with notes on nationalism, on seaside postcards, and on his own ambition – surely realized – to make political writing into an art.

and

BURMESE DAYS

HOMAGE TO CATALONIA

INSIDE THE WHALE AND OTHER ESSAYS

THE ROAD TO WIGAN PIER

THE COLLECTED ESSAYS, JOURNALISM AND LETTERS OF GEORGE ORWELL
(in four volumes)
Edited by Sonia Orwell and Ian Angus